THE GENOME PROJECT

The Evolution Gene Book I

AARON HODGES

Edited by Genevieve Lerner
Proofread by Sara Houston
Illustration by Deranged Doctor Designs

ABOUT THE AUTHOR

Aaron Hodges was born in 1989 in the small town of Whakatane, New Zealand. He studied for five years at the University of Auckland, completing a Bachelors of Science in Biology and Geography, and a Masters of Environmental Engineering. After working as an environmental consultant for two years, he grew tired of office work and decided to quit his job in 2014 and see the world. One year later, he published his first novel - Stormwielder.

FOLLOW AARON HODGES...
And receive TWO FREE novels and a short story!
www.aaronhodges.co.nz/newsletter-signup/

For the child inside us all.
Let them soar.

❧ I ❧
APPLICANTS

1

"Another pint, hun?"

Liz gritted her teeth as a man's voice carried to her from across the bar. Sucking in a breath, she forced a smile to her lips and looked around for the speaker. She found him sitting alone at a table in the corner, a drunken grin stretching across his unshaven cheeks. He caught her gaze and waved his empty mug.

Taking care to keep the smile plastered to her face, Liz walked across the diner to take his order.

"Just the beer, sir?" she asked, taking his mug. "It's last call."

He squinted at her as though struggling to understand her words. He was swaying slightly in his chair, and Liz was quite sure he'd already had enough. Unfortunately, her manager, Andrew, was never one to refuse a paying customer.

Finally, the man belched and waved the glass at her stomach. "What else is on the menu, love?"

He said the words with a leer that made Liz want to rip the mug from his hand and smash it over his head. Instead, all she did was smile sweetly. "Just the usual," she said, trying to keep the anger from her voice. "Kitchen is closed, though."

"Not interested in the kitchen." He leaned forward in his chair, and the stench of garlic and cigarettes wafted over Liz. "But I always wanted a taste of something rural."

Liz's stomach churned, and in a flash of anger she snatched the glass from the man's grease-stained fingers. Then, steeling herself, she took a breath, and forced a laugh. "Grass Valley Ale it is!"

Without waiting for a response, she spun on her heel and strode back through the maze of tables. Her neck prickled as she sensed his gaze on her, but she did not glance back. Retreating behind the bar, she added the dirty glass to the growing stack of dishes she had to tackle after closing, and took a fresh one from beneath the bar.

Liz paused as she turned and caught the man's beady eyes watching her from the corner. He had to be at least forty—more than twice her own seventeen years. Steadfastly ignoring his gaze, she poured out a pint of Grass Valley Ale.

"Keeping our guests happy I hope, Liz?" She jumped as Andrew appeared beside her.

At six-foot-five with a buzz cut and heavily built shoulders, Andrew towered over Liz's meagre five feet and two inches. He had served five years with the Western Allied States military before retiring from active duty and starting his own bar here in Sacramento. Or so he claimed on the memoire plastered on the back of every menu. It wasn't like there was any way to verify his story—even in the city, computers and the internet were only accessible to the rich. Where she'd grown up, they'd been lucky just to have electricity.

Crossing his tattooed arms, Andrew raised an eyebrow. She quickly flicked off the tap and placed the pint on a serving tray. "He's just drunk, Andrew," she muttered. "Nothing I can't handle."

"I didn't say handle him," Andrew replied coldly. "I said keep him happy."

Liz swallowed as he stared down at her, but she stood her ground. "That's what the beer's for." She nodded at the mug, taking advantage of the opportunity to break eye contact. "I'd better not keep him waiting."

Snatching up the metal tray, she raced back out amongst the tables. The other customers ignored her as she made her way between them. There were only a few occupied tables left now, and she was the last waitress on duty. It was a Tuesday night and her remaining patrons were mostly men in their thirties and forties—too young to have fought in the war that had claimed so many of their fathers.

"One Grass Valley Ale," Liz announced cheerfully as she placed the beer in front of the dark-eyed man. "Is that the lot for the night?"

Without answering, the man swept up the beer and gulped half of it down in a single swallow. He let out a long sigh as he placed it back on the table. "I like the taste." Before she could react, his arm shot out and wrapped around her waist. "Matter of fact, it's made me hungry for the real thing." He laughed as he dragged her forward.

Liz's heart dropped into the pit of her stomach as she felt his hand grasping her backside. The awful stench of his breath smothered her. Puckering up his lips, he tried to kiss her. She twisted away, the tray still clutched in one hand, and tried to shove him off. But even drunk, he was twice her size, and too strong to resist in such confined quarters.

"Get off," she snapped, the words grating up from the back of her throat.

"What? Think you're too good for me, ya little rural tramp?" His other hand came up, going for her breasts. "Come on, sweets, you know—"

Whatever he'd been about to say was cut off as Liz gripped her serving tray in both hands and brought it down on his head. A satisfying *clang* echoed through the room as it struck, and the hand vanished from around her waist.

The man reeled back in his chair, hands clutching at his face. Blood dribbled from a gash on his forehead, tangling with his greying hair. He lurched to his feet with a roar, sending the table and his freshly poured ale crashing to the ground. The sound of breaking glass was punctuated by his screams as Liz retreated a step, holding the tray in front of her like a shield. Her assailant swung his fists blindly in her direction, but alcohol had dimmed his senses and his blows met only empty air. Face beet red and cursing, he staggered in her direction.

"*Oy!*" Andrew's voice cut through the man's shouts like a knife.

Liz glanced back and saw him stepping out from behind the bar, the baseball bat he used to threaten rowdy customers grasped in hand.

"What's going on here?" he shouted as he marched towards them. The other patrons watched on, eyes wide, silent.

The drunkard took another step towards Liz before he seemed to catch himself. His eyes flickered uncertainly at Andrew, then back to her. "The little tramp *hit* me!"

Anger flickered in Liz's stomach. Throwing caution to the wind, she drew her lips back in a sneer. "Why don't you call me that one more time?" she growled, flourishing the tray.

Before her assailant had a chance to answer, Andrew caught Liz by the collar and hauled her back. She cried out as the tray slipped from her fingers and landed on her foot. Cursing, she staggered sideways, but before she could regain her balance, Andrew shoved her again, sending her crashing into an empty table.

"*Out!*" Andrew screamed, waving his bat above his head.

Liz scrambled back across the wooden floor, feeling the dried beer sticking to her clothes. Once out of range of his bat, she picked herself up and stood facing him. Heat rushed to her face. She struggled to keep from shaking as she clenched her fists.

"*What?*" she said through gritted teeth.

"I said *out!*" Andrew repeated, pointing the bat at her chest. "I've had enough of you. Your lot aren't worth the trouble."

Now Liz really was shaking. She opened her mouth to argue, and then snapped it closed again. Glancing around the room, she saw the eyes of everyone watching her. Ice spread through her chest as she looked back at her boss.

"What about my pay?" She tried to keep her voice as calm as possible.

"Consider it compensation for the damages." Sneering, he took a step towards her, until the bat prodded her in the chest.

Stomach twisting, Liz considered standing her ground. She needed that money—especially after the attention she had just attracted. She would have to move again now, pack her things and leave the room she'd already paid a month in advance for. With only the measly tips she'd made earlier in the night, she wouldn't have the cash for another room.

But she could see this was not a fight she was going to win. Letting out a long breath, she flicked a strand of curly black hair from her eyes and snorted. "Good riddance," she spat.

Spinning on her heel, she headed for the door. Her face burned as half a dozen eyes followed her. As she passed the last table, she paused, then lurched sideways, upending its contents onto the floor. The two men sitting there shouted and jumped to their feet as beer splattered them. By the time they turned their attention on her, Liz was already gone.

Outside, Liz blinked, struggling with the sudden darkness. The bar had no windows facing the road, and with the streetlight out front broken, it took a moment for her eyes to adjust. Not knowing if anyone was going to come after her, she quickly started off along the street, her hands still trembling with pent-up rage.

"Hope you enjoy cleaning up," she muttered under her breath.

Internally though, she cursed herself, even as she tried to contrive a plan that didn't involve sleeping on the streets for the rest of winter. Staying in this suburb was no longer an option—not after the commotion she'd just caused. Even though Andrew had been paying her under the table, it wouldn't take long for rumors to spread about the ferocious rural girl he'd employed. Then it would only be a matter of time before someone came asking questions.

Taking the next street on her right, Liz disappeared into the shadows between the buildings. She was on the outskirts of Sacramento, California, where the streets were still relatively quiet, free of the traffic clogging the center. Even so, she could never quite feel comfortable in a city. The countryside was her home—as everyone here was quick to remind her—but there was no work for her there. And while she could get by on what she trapped and scavenged in the summer, she couldn't stand the thought of another winter exposed to the icy elements.

So at the first whiff of cold, Liz had packed up her rucksack and headed for Sacramento. It was a long way from her hometown, but she was terrified anywhere closer might raise suspicions, make it easier for them to find her.

Until now, she had thought she'd made the right choice. From the tips she'd scraped together at the bar, she'd managed to rent what amounted to a closet in the basement of an apartment building. It was cold and damp, containing nothing more than a moldy mattress, but it was better than being woken up by falling snow. And it was off the books, too —safe.

But winter was barely a month old, and she'd

already blown it. Her teeth chattered as a cold wind whirled down the street, and Liz cursed herself for leaving her hole-ridden coat back in the bar. There would be no going back for it now. Scowling, she shoved her hands into the tiny pockets of her jeans and did her best to ignore the cold.

Liz glanced around again as she passed beneath a flickering streetlight. The urbanites could say whatever they liked about their shining condos—she still felt safer wandering the streets of any rural village than she did here. While she hadn't been troubled yet, she now kept a knife in her boot at all times. It paid to be prepared.

Unseen clouds blacked out the moon and stars, and the next streetlamp was a good two hundred yards away. Liz's heart started to race as the darkness pressed in around her. She picked up the pace, berating herself for her paranoia.

Reaching the next corner, Liz let out a long breath as she realized it was her street. Preoccupied, she'd lost track of the turns, but somehow had still ended up in the right place. Pulling her hands from her pockets, she power-walked towards the cul-de-sac at the end of the lane. Her apartment building was dark, and the only illumination was a flickering streetlight hovering above the turnabout.

Halfway down her street, Liz caught the faintest whisper of something behind her. Goosebumps shot down her neck, and she looked back slowly, expecting to see a stray dog wandering across the road…

…and screamed as a shadow rushed towards her.

Adrenaline kicked in as the man lunged, and she lurched back, hearing the *whoosh* as a fist shot past her head. A curse followed, then the weight of his body crashed into her. But she was ready now, already pivoting on her heel, allowing his bulk to slide by her. The man staggered past, and she leapt, driving her foot into the small of his back to send him toppling to the ground.

Then she was sprinting away, eyes fixed on the light at the end of the lane, and the iron door to her apartment building. If she could just make it inside…

Liz barely managed five steps before two men emerged from the shadows ahead, cutting off her escape. She staggered to a stop as they started towards her. Neither spoke, but they moved with a deliberate calm, as though they had all the time in the world to catch her.

Ice spread through Liz's veins as she turned to flee back down the lane, and found her first attacker on his feet, barring the way. For an instant she froze, her insides turning to liquid, panic taking hold. But it only lasted a second—there was no time for hesitation out on the streets.

Dropping to one knee, she inconspicuously slipped the knife from her boot, and then leapt at the first man. A low growl rumbled from her throat as her anger took light. It had already been a bad night —she wasn't about to let these thugs make it worse.

The man hadn't seen her knife. His teeth gleamed in the light of the distant lamp as he smiled and opened his arms to catch her. The next second, he was staggering backwards, eyes blinking rapidly as he reached for the blade embedded in his chest.

Sneering at his surprise, Liz tried to yank back her weapon, but he sagged to the ground before she could dislodge it. She cursed, wasting half a second considering going after it, and then leapt free—only for his thrashing arms to take her legs out from under her. She crashed into the asphalt, her bones jarring at the impact. Fabric tore around her knees as she scrambled back to her feet.

She tried to run again, but the other two were on her now. A hand caught Liz's hair and pulled her backwards. Screaming, she twisted and swung at her assailant. Her fist went wide as the man leaned back, but her second blow caught him square in the throat. He staggered, but his grip didn't falter, and Liz shrieked as she was dragged down with him.

Tears sprang to her eyes as she yanked back her head and felt a clump of hair tear free. Something wet and sticky trickled down her skull, but she ignored it and tried to regain her feet.

A cry tore from her lips as the last assailant tacked her from behind. The breath rushed from her chest as his weight drove her face first into the ground. Choking, she thrashed beneath him, trying to break free, to gulp in a mouthful of air, but his weight pinned her down. Stars streaked her vision as she gasped, and finally managed to suck in a breath.

"Doctor," came the man's voice from right above her head, followed by the crackle of a radio. "We have her."

"On my way, Commander," a woman's tinny voice replied.

Liz's blood chilled at the voice. This was no drunken attack, no crime of opportunity. They had been waiting for *her*. Sucking in another half breath, she managed to croak out a pathetic cry for help. Iron fingers dug into the base of her neck and ground her face into the asphalt.

"Quiet," her captor growled.

Liz stilled, even as her mind went into overdrive, seeking a way out. Her ears twitched as a distant *tap-tapping* echoed along the street. Her heart soared as she recognized the sound of footsteps. She cried out again, louder now, and received a blow to her head for the effort. Stars swirled in her vision again as the strength fled her limbs.

"Enough of that," a woman's voice came from overhead.

For a second, Liz thought someone had heard her calls.

"Yes, Doctor," her captor replied.

Liz's hope crumbled to dust as she realized the footsteps belonged to the woman from the radio.

"You're sure she's the one?" the woman asked.

"Matches the photograph," came the reply.

"Excellent."

The sound of leather scuffing against concrete followed. Cracking open her eyes, Liz saw a sleek black pair of women's shoes beside her face. Presumably they belonged to the doctor, but Liz could see nothing more of the woman.

"Please," Liz managed to croak, "you've got to help me. You've got the wrong girl."

Neither of her captives deigned to reply. In her heart, Liz knew her words were a lie, that her past had finally caught up with her. She'd thought she'd covered her tracks so well, moving around, shifting from town to town, using a fake name, keeping off the records. On her brightest days, she'd thought they might have finally stopped looking, that they'd given up.

How naive she'd been.

She flinched as something cold pressed against her neck. Gas hissed and she felt a sharp pinch, then the pressure was gone. But now a strange warmth was spreading slowly down her spine, numbing as it went, and she realized they'd injected her with something.

Liz knew it was hopeless, that it was already too late and the drug would soon render her unconscious, but she thrashed all the same. The man holding her swore and his grip on her neck tightened, hurting her. She cursed him, calling them every filthy word she could remember, but it was no use. He had her pinned on her stomach and there was nothing she could do to free herself.

Then suddenly, the iron fingers were gone, the weight on her back vanished. Hope swelled in Liz's chest, and she struggled to sit up, to scramble to her feet and race down the lane—back to the bar, to the cold, to the countryside, anywhere but these men and the doctor.

Instead, she found her limbs twitching uselessly, her body unresponsive, her mind falling away into a swirling darkness.

Too late, she opened her mouth to scream.

2

Chris let out a long sigh as he settled into the worn-out sofa, then cursed as a broken spring stabbed him in the backside. Wriggling sideways to avoid it, he reached for the remote, only to realize it had been left beside the television. Muttering under his breath, he climbed back to his feet, retrieved the remote, flicked on the television, and finally collapsed back into the sofa. This time he was careful to avoid the broken spring.

He closed his eyes as the blue glow of the television lit the living room. The shriek of commercials followed, but he barely had the energy to be annoyed. He was still at school, but he'd had to take on an afternoon job at the construction site down the road to help his mother make ends meet. Even with the extra income, they were struggling. His only hope was passing the entrance exams for the California State

University and winning a scholarship. Otherwise, he would have to beg his supervisor for an apprenticeship.

"Another attack was reported today from the rural town of Julian." A reporter's voice broke through the stream of adverts, announcing the start of the six o'clock news.

Chris's ears perked up and he looked quickly at the television. Images flashed across the screen of an old mining town, its dusty dirt roads and rundown buildings looking unchanged since the 1900's. A row of horse-drawn carriages lined the street, their owners standing alongside them.

It was a common sight in the rural counties of the Western Allied States. The divide between rural and urban communities had grown in the thirty years since California, Oregon and Washington had declared their independence from the United States. Today, there were few citizens in the countryside able to afford luxuries such as cars and televisions.

"We're just receiving word that the police have arrived on the scene," the reporter continued.

On the television, a black van with the letters SWAT painted on the side had just pulled up. The rear doors swung open, and a squad of black-garbed riot police leapt out. They gathered around the van and then strode on past the carriages. Dust swirled around them, but they moved without hesitation, the camera following them at a distance.

The image changed as the police moved around a corner into an empty street. The new camera angle looked down at the police from the rooftop of a nearby building. It followed the SWAT unit as they split into two groups and spread out along the street, rifles at the ready.

Then the camera panned down the street and refocused on the broken window of a grocery store. The camera zoomed, revealing the nightmare inside the store.

Chris swallowed as images straight from a horror film flashed across the television. The remnants of the store lay scattered across the linoleum floor, the contents of broken cans and wine bottles staining the ground red. Pieces of humanity were scattered amongst the wreckage, torn arms and shattered legs lying apart from their motionless owners. Chris's stomach twisted as he looked into the eyes of the dead and saw the terror of their final moments reflected back at him.

Finally the camera tilted and panned to the sole survivor of the carnage. The man stood amidst the wreckage of the store, blood streaking his face and arms, staining his shirt red. His head was bowed, and the only sign of life was the rhythmic rise and fall of his shoulders. The camera zoomed in on his face, revealing cold grey eyes. They stared at the ground, blank and lifeless.

Struggling to contain the meagre contents of his stomach, Chris looked away.

"The *Chead* is thought to have awakened at around sixteen hundred hours," the reporter was saying now, drawing Chris back to the screen. "Special forces have cleared the immediate area and are now preparing to engage with the creature."

"Two hours." Chris jumped up as a woman's voice came from behind him.

He spun on his heel, then relaxed as his mother walked in from the kitchen. "I thought you had a night class!" he gasped.

His mother shook her head, a slight smile touching her face. "We finished early." She shrugged, then waved at the television. "They've been standing around for two hours. Watching that thing. Some of those people were still alive when it all started. They might have been saved. Would have, if they'd been somebody important."

Chris pulled himself off the couch and embraced his mother. He kissed her cheek and she returned the gesture, before they both turned to watch the SWAT team approach the grocery store. The men in black moved with military precision, jogging down the dirt road, sticking close to the buildings. If the *Chead* came out of its trance, no one wanted to be caught in the open. While the creatures looked human, they possessed a terrifying speed, and had the strength to tear full-grown men limb from limb.

As the scene inside the grocery store demonstrated.

Absently, Chris clutched his mother's arm tighter. The *Chead* were a curse throughout the Western Allied States, or WAS as many called them, a dark shadow left over from the days of the American War. The first whispers of the creatures had started in 2030, not long after the fall of the United States. They had been dismissed then as a rumor, the new country eager to move on from the decade-long conflict. Attacks had been blamed on resistance fighters in rural communities, who had never fully supported the severance from the United States.

In response, the government had imposed curfews in the affected counties, and sent in the military to quell the unrest. But their measures had done nothing to stem the attacks, and eventually, accounts by survivors had filtered through to the media. Claims surfaced that it was not soldiers behind the butchery, but members of the community. The perpetrators were always different, but the story was the same. One day the assailants were ordinary neighbors or colleagues – the next, monsters capable of tearing their loved ones to pieces.

By the time the first creature was captured, rural communities had suffered almost a decade of terror at the hands of the monstrosities. The government and their media agencies had pointed the blame in every direction, from poor rural police-reporting, to secret operations by the Texans to destabilize the Western Allied States.

On the television, the SWAT team had reached the grocery store and were now gathering outside, their rifles trained on the entrance. One lowered his rifle and stepped towards it, the others covering him from behind. Reaching the door, he stretched out an arm to pull it open.

The *Chead* didn't make a sound as it tore through the store windows and barreled into the man. A screech came through the old television speakers as the men scattered before the creature's ferocity. With one hand, the creature grabbed its victim by the throat and hurled him across the street. The *thud* as he bounced off a concrete wall was audible over the reporter's microphone.

The sight of their companion's untimely demise seemed to snap the other members of the squadron into action. The first pops of gunfire followed, but the *Chead* was already on the move. It tore across the dirt road, bullets raising dust-clouds around it, and smashed into another squad member. A scream echoed up from the street as man and *Chead* went down, disappearing into a cloud of dust.

Despite the risk of hitting their comrade, the other members of the SWAT team did not stop firing. The chance of survival once a *Chead* had its hands on you was zero to none, and no one wanted to risk the creature escaping.

Roaring, the *Chead* reared up from the dust, then spun as a bullet struck it in the shoulder. Blood blossomed from the wound as it staggered back, its grey eyes wide, flickering with surprise. It reached up and touched a finger to the hole left by the bullet, its brow creasing with confusion.

Then the rest of the men opened fire, and the creature fell.

3

Doctor Angela Fallow squinted through the rain-streaked windshield, struggling to catch a glimpse of her subject in the lengthening gloom. A few minutes ago the streetlights had flickered into life, but despite their yellowed glow, shadows still clung to the house across the street. Tall hedges marked the boundary with the neighboring properties, while a white picket fence stood between her car and the old cottage.

Leaning closer to the window, Angela held her breath to keep the glass from fogging, and willed her eyes to pierce the twilight. But beyond the brightly-lit sidewalk, she could see nothing but darkness. Letting out a long sigh, she sat back in her seat. There was no sign of anyone outside the house, no silent shadows slipping closer to the warm light beckoning from the windows.

At least, no sign that could be seen.

Berating her nerves, Angela turned her attention to the touchscreen on her dashboard. She had no wish to see a repeat of the casualties her team had suffered in Sacramento. She cursed as the soft glow of the screen lit the car, before she remembered the tinted windows made it impossible for anyone to see inside.

Angela pursed her lips, studying the charts on the screen one last time. It showed a woman in her early forties. Auburn hair hung around her shoulders and she wore the faintest hint of a smile on her red lips. The smile spread to her cheeks, crinkling the skin around her olive-green eyes.

Margaret Sanders.

Beneath the picture was a description of the woman: height, weight, license number, last known address, school and work history, her current occupation as a college professor, and marital status. The last was listed as widowed with a single child. Her husband had succumbed to cancer almost a decade previously.

Shaking her head, Angela looked again at the woman's eyes, wondering what could have driven her to this end. She had a house, a son, solid employment as a teacher. Why would she throw it all away when she had so much to lose?

Idly, she wondered whether Mrs. Sanders would have done things differently if given another chance.

The smile lines around her eyes were those of a kind soul, and her alleged support of the resistance seemed out of character. It was a shame the government did not give second chances—especially not for traitors of the state.

Now both mother and son would suffer for her actions.

Tapping the screen, Angela pulled up the son's file. Christopher Sanders, at eighteen, was the reason she had come tonight. The assault team would handle the mother and any of her associates who might be on the property, but Angela had other plans for the son. Like the rest of her subjects, he would need to be taken alive—and unharmed.

His profile described him as five-foot-eleven, with a weight of 150 pounds—not large by any measure. Her only concern was the black belt listed in his credentials, though such accomplishments were rarely relevant when it came to a real fight. Particularly when the target was unarmed, unsuspecting, and outnumbered.

Then again, the girl had given them more trouble than anyone had expected.

Forcing her mind back to the present, Angela tapped the screen again, and a picture of her target popped up. A flicker of discomfort spread through her stomach. His brunette hair showed traces of his mother's auburn locks, while the hazel eyes must have descended from a dominant *bey2* allele in his father's chromosome. A hint of light-brown facial hair traced the edges of his jaw, covering the last of his teenage acne. Despite his small size, he had the broad, muscular shoulders of an athlete, and there was little sign of fat on his youthful face.

After a long moment, Angela flicked off the console. She hoped this would be her final assignment. For months now, she had overseen the collection of subjects for the new trials, and the task had not gotten any easier with time. The children she'd taken haunted her at night, their accusing stares waiting whenever she closed her eyes. Her only consolation was that without her, these children would have suffered the same fate as their parents. At least the research facility gave them a fighting chance.

And looking into the boy's eyes, she knew he was a fighter.

Angela closed her eyes, and shoving aside her doubt, she pressed another button on the car's console.

"Are you in position?" she spoke into the empty car.

"Ready when you are, Fallow," a man replied.

Nodding to herself, Fallow reached beneath her seat and retrieved a steel briefcase. Unclipping its restraints, she lifted out a jet injector and held it up to the light. The stainless-steel instrument appeared more like a gun than a piece of medical equipment, but it served its purpose well. Once her team had Chris restrained, it would be a simple matter to use the jet injector to anesthetize the young man for transport.

Removing a vial of etorphine from the case, she screwed it into place and pressed a button on the side. A short *hiss* confirmed it was pressurized. She eyed the clear liquid, hoping the details in the boy's file were correct. She had prepared the dosage of etorphine for Chris's age and weight, but a miscalculation could prove fatal.

"Fallow, still waiting on your signal?" the voice came again.

Fallow bit her lip and closed her eyes. She shivered in the cold of the car.

If not you, then someone else.

She opened her eyes. "Go."

❧ 4 ❧

The screen of the old CRT television flickered to black as Chris's mother switched it off. Her face was pale when she turned towards him, and a shiver ran through her.

"Your grandfather would be ashamed, Chris," she said, shaking her head. "He went to war against the United States because he believed in this country, because thought we could be the light to the madness that had overcome the old union. He fought to keep us free, not to spend decades haunted by the ghosts of our past."

Chris shuddered. He'd never met his grandfather, but his mother and grandmother talked of him enough that Chris felt he knew him. When the United States had refused to accept the independence of the Western Allied States, his grandfather had answered the call to defend their young nation.

Enlisting with the WAS Marines, he'd marched off to a conflict that had quickly expanded to engulf the whole of North America. Only the aid of Canada and Mexico had given the WAS the strength to survive, and eventually prevail against the aggression of the United States. Unfortunately, Chris's grandfather had not.

"Things will change soon," Chris said. "Surely?"

His mother crinkled her nose. "I've been saying that for ten years," she said as she moved towards the kitchen, ruffling Chris's hair as she passed him, "but things only ever seem to get worse."

Chris followed her and pulled out a chair at the wooden table. The kitchen was small, barely big enough for the two of them, but it was all they needed. His mother was already standing at the stove, stirring a pot of stew he recognized as leftovers from the beef shanks of the night before.

"Most don't seem to care, as long as the attacks are confined to the countryside," Chris commented.

"Exactly." His mother turned, emphatically waving the wooden spoon. "They think it doesn't matter, that their shining cities will protect them. Well, it won't stay that way forever."

"No." Chris shook his head. "That one in Seattle…" He shuddered. Over fifty people had been killed when a *Chead* woke in a shopping mall. Police had arrived in less than ten minutes, but that was all the time it had needed.

Impulsively, he reached for the pocket watch he wore around his neck. His mother had given it to him ten years ago, at his father's funeral. It held a picture of Chris's parents, smiling on the shores of Lake Washington in Seattle, where they'd first met. His heart gave a painful throb as he thought of the terror engulfing the city.

Noticing the gesture, his mother abandoned the pot and pulled him into a hug. "It's okay, Chris. We'll survive this. We're a strong people. They'll come up with a solution, even if we have to march up to the gates of congress and demand it."

Chris nodded, and was about to speak when a crash came from somewhere in the house. They pushed apart and spun towards the kitchen doorway. Though they lived in the city, they barely had the money to survive week to week, and their house was not in the safest neighborhood.

It was well past the eight o'clock curfew now. Whoever—or whatever—had made the noise was not likely to be friendly.

Sucking in a breath, Chris moved into the doorway and risked a glance across the lounge. The single incandescent bulb cast shadows across the room, leaving dark patches behind the couch and television. He stared hard into the darkness, searching for signs of movement, and then retreated to the kitchen.

Silently, his mother handed him a kitchen knife.

He took it after only a second's hesitation. She held a second blade in a practiced grip. Looking at his mother's face, Chris swallowed. Her eyes were hard, her brow creased in a scowl, but he did not miss the fear there. Together they faced the door—and waited.

The squeak of the loose floorboard in the hallway seemed as loud as a gunshot in the silent house. Chris glanced at his mother, and she nodded back. There was no doubt now. Someone was inside.

A crash came from the lounge, then the thud of heavy boots as the intruder gave up all pretense of stealth. Chris tensed, his knuckles turning white as he gripped the knife handle. He spread his feet into a forward stance, readying himself.

The sound of breaking glass came from their right as the kitchen window exploded inwards, and a black-suited figure leapt into the room. The man bowled into his mother, sending her tumbling to the ground before she could swing the knife. Chris sprang to the side as another man charged from the lounge, then drew back and hurled his knife.

Without pausing to see whether the blade struck home, Chris twisted and leapt, driving his heel into the midriff of the intruder standing over his mother. But the man was ready for him, and with his greater bulk, he brushed off the blow. Stumbling sideways, Chris clenched his fists and charged again.

The man grinned, raising his hands to catch

Chris. With his attention diverted, Chris's mother rose behind him, knife still in hand, and drove the blade deep into their attacker's hamstring.

Their black-garbed attacker barely had time to scream before Chris's fist slammed into his windpipe. The intruder's face paled and his hands went to his throat. He staggered backwards, strangled noises gurgling from his mouth, and toppled over the kitchen table.

Chris offered his mother a hand. Before she could take it, a creak came from the floorboards behind him. The man from the lounge loomed up, grabbing Chris by the shoulder. Still on the ground, his mother rolled away as Chris twisted around, fighting to break the man's hold. Cursing, he aimed an elbow at the man's gut, but his arm struck solid body armor and bounced off.

The body armor explained what had happened to the knife Chris had thrown, but before he could process what the information meant, another crash came from the window.

His mother surged to her feet as a third man leapt inside. Still holding the bloodied knife, she screamed and charged. Straining his arms, Chris bucked against his captor's grip, but there was no breaking the man's iron hold. Stomach clenched, he watched his mother attack the heavily-armed assailant.

The new intruder carried a steel baton in one

hand, and as she swung her knife it flashed out and caught her wrist. His mother screamed, and the blade tumbled from her hand. She retreated across the room, cradling her arm. A fourth man appeared in the doorway to the lounge. Before Chris could shout a warning, he grabbed her from behind.

His mother shrieked and threw back her head, trying to catch the man in the chin, but her blows bounced off his body armor. Her eyes widened as his arm went around her neck, cutting off her breath. Heart hammering in his chest, Chris twisted and kicked at his opponent's shins, desperate to aid his mother, but the man showed no sign of relenting.

"*Mom!*" he screamed as her eyes drooped closed.

"Doctor Fallow, situation under control. You're up," the man from the window spoke into his cuff. He approached his wounded comrade, whose face was turning purple. "Hold on, man. Medical's on its way."

"Who are you?" Chris gasped.

The man ignored him. Instead, he went to work on the fallen man, removing his belt and binding it around the man's leg. The injured man groaned as the speaker worked, his eyes squeezed closed and his teeth clenched. A pang of guilt touched Chris, but he crushed it down.

"What the hell happened?" a woman exclaimed as she entered the kitchen.

The woman was dark-skinned, but the color was

rapidly fleeing her face as she looked around the kitchen. She raised a hand to her mouth, her eyes lingering on the blood, then flicking between the men and their captives. Shock showed in their amber depths, but already it was fading as she reasserted control. Lowering her hand to her side, she pursed her red lips. Her gaze settled on Chris.

A chill went through him as he noticed the red-emblazoned bear on the front of her black jacket. The symbol marked her as a government employee. These were not random thugs in the night. They were the police, and they were here for Chris and his mother.

Nodding to herself, the woman reached into her jacket and drew something into the light. The breath caught in Chris's throat as he glimpsed the contraption in her hand. For a second he thought it was a pistol, but as she drew closer he realized his mistake. It was some sort of hypodermic gun, some device he'd only thought existed in old movies. In real life though, it was far more terrifying than anything Hollywood had ever produced.

"Who are you?" Chris croaked as she paused in front of him.

Her eyes drifted to Chris's face, but she only shook her head. She studied the liquid in the vial attached to the gun's barrel, then looked back at Chris, as though weighing him up.

"Hold him," she said at last.

"What?" Chris gasped as his captor pulled his arms behind his back. "What are you doing? Please, you're making a mistake, we haven't done anything wrong!"

The woman didn't answer. Chris struggled to escape as she raised the gun to his neck, but the man only pulled his arms harder, sending a bolt of pain through his shoulders. Biting back a scream, Chris looked up at the woman. Their eyes met, and he thought he saw a flicker of regret in her eyes.

Then the cold of the hypodermic gun touched his neck, followed by a hiss of gas as she pressed the trigger. Metal pinched Chris's neck, and then the woman stepped back. Holding his breath, Chris stared at the woman, his eyes never leaving hers.

Within seconds, the first touch of weariness started to seep through Chris's body. He blinked as shadows spread around the edges of his vision. Idly, he struggled to free his arms, so he might chase the shadows away. But the man still held him fast. Sucking in a mouthful of air, Chris fought against the exhaustion. Blinking hard, he willed himself to resist the pull of sleep.

But there was no stopping the warmth spreading through his limbs. His head bobbed and his arms went limp, until the only thing keeping him upright was the strength of his captor.

The woman's face was the last thing Chris saw before he slipped into the darkness.

5

Liz shivered as the air conditioner hummed, sending a blast of icy air in her direction. Wrapping her arms around herself, she closed her eyes and waited for it to pass. The scent of chlorine drifted on the air, its chemical reek setting her head to pounding. Her teeth chattered and she shuddered as the whir of fans died away. Groaning, Liz opened her eyes and returned to studying her surroundings.

She had woken ten minutes ago in this thirty-foot-wide concrete room. A single door stood closed on the opposite wall, a small glass panel revealing a bright hallway beyond. It appeared to be the only exit, but it might as well have been half a world away. Between Liz and the door stood the wire mesh of her five-foot by five-foot steel cage.

Trembling, Liz gripped the wire tight between her fingers and leaned her head against it. She tried to search the vaults of her memory, to recall how she had come to be there, but her last recollection was of serving beer to a drunken customer in Andrew's pub.

A curse slipped from her lips as the blast of the air conditioner returned. Without her jacket, her clothes were no match for whatever freezing temperature the climate control had been set to. To make matters worse, her boots were gone, and the concrete was like ice beneath her feet.

At least I'm not alone, she thought wryly, looking through the wire into the cage beside her.

A young man somewhere around her own eighteen years lay there, still dozing on the concrete floor. His clothes were better kept than her own, though there was a bloodstain on one sleeve. From the quality of his shirt, she guessed he was from the city. Pale skin, untouched by the scorching heat of the countryside, only served to confirm her suspicions.

Groaning, the young man began to stir. Idly, Liz wondered what he'd make of the nightmare into which he was about to awaken.

She shivered, not from the cold now, but dread. Casting her eyes around the room, she sought one last time for something, *anything*, that might offer escape. Long ago, her parents had warned her of the fate destined for those who drew the government's ire. Though never reported, disappearances had been common in her community. Adults, children, even entire families were known to simply disappear overnight. Few were brave enough to voice their suspicions out loud, but everyone knew who'd taken them.

It seemed after two years on the run, those same people had finally caught up with Liz.

The clang of the door as it opened tore Liz from her thoughts. She watched as two men pushed their way past the heavy steel door and stepped into the room. They wore matching uniforms of black pants and green shirts, and the gold- and red-embossed badges of bears on their chests confirmed Liz's suspicions—she'd been taken by government soldiers. The men were armed with rifles and moved with the casual ease of professional killers.

Liz straightened as their eyes alighted on her, refusing to show her fear. She suppressed a shudder as broad grins split their faces. Fixing a scowl to her lips, she crossed her arms and stared them down.

"Feisty one, ain't she?" the first said in a strong Californian accent. Shaking his head, he walked past the twin cages to a panel in the wall.

"Looks like the boy's still asleep," the second commented. "Gonna be a nasty wake-up."

Together, the men opened the panel and retrieved a hose. Thick nylon strings encased the outer layer of the hose, and a large steel nozzle was fitted to its end. Dragging it across the room, they pointed it at the sleeping boy and flipped a lever on the nozzle.

Water gushed from the hose and through the wire of the cage, engulfing the unconscious young man. A bloodcurdling scream echoed off the walls, and he seemed to levitate off the floor. Another cry followed as he thrashed against the torrent.

Liz bit back laughter as his scream turned into a gurgle. The men with the hose showed no such restraint, and their laughter echoed loudly in the confined space. Ignoring the young man's strangled cries, they held the water steady until it seemed he could not help but drown in the rushing water.

When they finally shut off the nozzle, the boy collapsed to the floor of his cage, gasping for breath. He shuddered, spitting up water, but the men were already moving towards Liz, and she had no more time to consider his predicament.

She raised her hands as the men stopped in front of her cage. "No need for that, boys. I'm already clean, see?" She did a little turn, her cheeks warming as she sensed their eyes on her again.

The men chuckled, but shook their heads. "Sorry girl, boss's orders."

They pulled the lever before Liz could muster up any other arguments.

Liz shrieked as the ice-cold water drove her back against the rear of the cage. She lifted her hands in front of her face, fighting to breathe, but it made little difference against the rush. Gasping, she choked as water flooded down her throat, and fell to her knees. An icy hand seemed to grip her chest as she inhaled again, turning away to protect her face. The power of the water forced her up against the wire, and she gripped it hard, struggling to hold herself upright.

When the torrent finally ceased, Liz found herself crouched on the ground with her back to the men. She did not turn as a coughing fit shook her body. An awful cold seeped into her bones as she struggled for breath. Water filled her ears and nose, muffling the words of the men, until she shook her head to clear it.

Tightening her hold on the wire, Liz used it to pull herself to her feet. Head down, she gave a final cough and faced the room.

The men were already returning the hose to its panel in the wall. They spoke quietly amongst themselves, but fell silent as the hinges squeaked again. A group of men and women entered the room. There were five in total, three men and two women. Each wore a white lab coat with black pants, and golden bears pinned to their collars. Four carried electronic tablets, their attention on the little screens, while the fifth approached the guards. They straightened as he stopped up in front of them, their grins turning to staunch grimaces.

"Are our latest subjects ready for processing?" the man asked, his voice cool.

One of the guards nodded. "Yes, Doctor Halt. We just finished hosing them down."

Halt smiled. "Very good." He dismissed the men with a flick of his hand and turned to face the cages.

Pursing thin lips, Halt paced around Liz's cage in a slow circle. His grey eyes never left her as he completed the circuit, and eventually she was forced to look away. He watched her like a predator studying its prey, eyeing up which piece of flesh to taste first. Wrapping her arms around herself, Liz fixed her eyes to the concrete and tried to ignore him.

When she looked up again, Halt had moved on to the young man in the other cage. But her fellow captive was ignoring the doctor, and was instead staring at the group of people in lab coats. His brow creased, as though struggling to recall a distant memory.

"*You!*" the boy shouted suddenly, slamming his hands against the wire. "You were at my house! What am I doing here? *What have you done with my mother?*"

Halt frowned, glancing back at the group of doctors. "Doctor Fallow, would you care to explain why the subject knows your face?"

The woman at the head of the group turned beet-red. "There were complications during his extraction, Halt." She spoke softly, but there was a challenge beneath her words. Goosebumps spread down Liz's spine as she recognized the voice, though she could not recall from where. "I had to enter before the subject was fully secured, or we risked further casualties amongst the extraction team."

Halt eyed her for a moment, apparently weighing up her words, before nodding. "Very well." He turned back to the cages. "No matter. Elizabeth Flores, Christopher Sanders, welcome to your new home."

Icy fear gripped Liz by the throat, silencing her voice. They knew her last name. That meant they knew who she was, where she came from. The last trickle of hope evaporated from her heart.

Christopher was not so easily quelled. "What am I doing here? You can't hold us like his, I know my rights—"

Halt raised a hand, and Liz's neighbor fell silent. Standing outside Christopher's cage, Halt stared through the wire. "Your mother has been charged with treason."

Color fled the boy's face, turning his skin a sickly yellow. He swallowed and opened his mouth, but no words came out. Tears crystallized at the corner of his eyes, but he blinked them back before they could fall.

Biting her tongue, Liz watched the two face off against one another. She was impressed by Christopher's resilience. He might speak with the accent of someone from the city, but he seemed to possess more courage than any of the boys she'd once known at her boarding school. If his mother had been accused of treason, it meant death for her and her family. The elderly would be afforded an exception, but her children...

Liz turned her attention to the group still lingering behind Halt. If that was the reason Christopher was here, she didn't like her chances. She had feared the authorities would come for her, and had done her best to avoid detection. But with government agents hiding behind every shadow, she had always known it was only a matter of when, not if, they found her. It seemed her time was finally up.

And yet, she needed to know: how much did these people truly know about her?

6

"What about me?" Liz croaked. "My parents are dead. I've done nothing wrong."

Halt's scowl deepened. "Elizabeth Flores." He paused, looking her up and down with a sneer. "Vagrant, beggar, fugitive. You have escaped justice for long enough. After what your parents did, did you really think we would not come for you? That we would not hunt you to the ends of the earth?"

White-hot fire lit in Liz's chest, but she forced herself to take a deep breath and swallow the scream building in her throat. She wanted to deny the accusations, to curse him and the others, but she knew there was no point. She had tried that once before, when they had first come for her. But one look at her ragged clothes, at the curly black hair and olive skin, and they had dismissed her words as lies.

Her shoulders slumped as Halt looked away.

Wrapping her arms around herself, she staggered to the back of the cage and sank to the floor. She wasn't giving up, not yet, but she knew when silence was the better course of action.

Unlike her fellow prisoner.

"What is this place?" Christopher's voice was soft, as though if he whispered, Halt's answer might offer some sort of mercy.

Liz glanced at him, watching as he lost the battle with his tears. Despite herself, sympathy swelled in her chest. She knew what it was like, to lose one's parents. She would not wish it on anyone.

"This is your redemption." Halt spread his arms, including them both in the gesture. "This is your chance to redress the crimes of your parents, to contribute to the betterment of our nation. The government has seen fit to offer you both a reprieve."

"How generous of them," Liz muttered from the floor.

She shivered as Halt's eyes found hers. They flashed with anger, offering a silent warning against further interruptions. Pursing her lips, she gripped the wire tighter. It cut into her fingers as she willed herself to remain silent.

"My mother was not a traitor," came Christopher's response. "How dare you—"

Halt waved a hand and the guards who still waited at the back of the room came to life. They marched past the silent group of doctors and approached Chris's cage. One produced a key, and a second later they had the door open. They moved inside, and a brief scuffle followed as they tried to get their hands on the boy. One staggered back from a blow to the face before the other managed to use his bulk to pin Christopher to the wire.

When both guards had a firm grip on him, they hauled Christopher out and forced him to his knees in front of Halt. The doctor loomed over the boy, arms folded. He contemplated Chris with empty eyes, like a spider studying a fly trapped in its web. Liz watched on in silence, hardly daring to breathe as Halt nodded to the guards.

The one on the left drew back his boot and slammed it into Christopher's stomach. He collapsed without a sound, mouth wide, gasping like a fish out of water. A low wheeze came from his throat as he rolled onto his back and strained for breath. It came with a sudden groan, before another boot crashed into his side, almost lifting him off the ground.

A scream tore from the young man's throat as he tried to roll into a ball. But the other guard only grabbed him by the scruff of his neck and hauled him back to his knees. The two of them looked at Halt then, waiting for further instruction.

Halt approached, one finger tapping idly against his elbow. Softly, he continued as though nothing had happened. "As I was saying, you have been given a reprieve. But the crimes of your parents still stand, as does the sentence on your lives. You no longer exist in the eyes of the state. You are no one, nothing but what we permit you to be. If you're lucky, we might find you worthy of our work here." Liz shivered. She had no idea what work Halt was talking about, but she had a feeling she wouldn't like it. "More likely though," Halt continued, "you will die. But know at least that your deaths will have advanced the interests of our fine nation."

Chris was still kneeling on the ground between the guards, his breath coming in ragged gasps. Halt eyed him, as though weighing whether his words had sunk in.

"In the meantime, you will respect and obey your betters," Halt murmured. "Soon, you will be shown to your new accommodation, but first, I want to be sure you understand the gravity of your situation. Christopher Sanders, why are you here?"

On the ground, Chris looked up at the doctor. His eyes shone, but no tears fell. Turning his head, he spat on the concrete. "She's a terrible cook." He coughed, then continued, "but that hardly makes her a traitor—"

The guard's fist caught him in the side of the head and sent him crashing to the floor. A kick followed, and for the next thirty seconds the thud of hard leather boots on flesh echoed through the room. When the guards finally retreated, the young man lay still, his soft moans the only sign of life.

"Get him up," Halt commanded.

Together, the guards hauled the boy back to his knees. This time Halt leaned down, until the two of them were face-to-face. "Well?"

Christopher's shoulders sagged. A sob came from him, and for a second Liz thought he would not speak. Then he nodded, a whisper following. "Okay," he croaked, "okay…my mother…is a traitor." He looked up as he finished, a spark of flame still burning in his eyes. "*Are you happy?*"

The doctor studied him for a long while, as though weighing up the admission alongside his show of defiance. Finally he nodded, and the guards grabbed Christopher by the shoulders and muscled him back into the cage.

The clang as the door closed sent a sliver of ice down Liz's spine. She stared at the floor, sensing the eyes of the room on her, and waited for Halt's words.

"Elizabeth Flores." His voice snaked its way around her, raising the hackles on her neck. "You have been on the run for a long time. Surely you, at least, must admit to your parents' crimes?"

Looking up, Liz found the cold grey eyes of the doctor watching her. She suppressed a shudder and quickly looked away. Taking slow, measured breaths, she beat down the rage burning in her chest. She took one step, then another, until she reached the front of her cage. Leaning against the wire, she looked at the doctor and raised an eyebrow.

"What would you like me to admit to?" she whispered.

Halt took a step back from the cage, but she did not miss the way his eyes lingered on her. She gave a little smirk as he growled. "Disgusting girl," he spat. "Admit that your parents were monsters—that you aided them, that for years you have run from the law, hiding from justice."

A tremor shook Liz and she bit her lip to keep from screaming at him. Closing her eyes, she sent out a silent prayer for the souls of her parents. Their faces drifted through her mind—smiling, happy, at peace. They had been kind and sweet, only ever wanting her to be happy, to have a better life than the one they'd lived. For years they had scraped and saved to send her to boarding school in the city. The day Liz had been accepted, she'd never seen them so happy. And for three years, she had suffered the taunts of her peers in that school to keep them that way.

But they were long gone; they didn't care what she said about them. There was no need for Liz to suffer, to bleed for their memory. Not now, when there was no hope of escape. But silently she made a vow: to bide her time and conserve her strength, until an opportunity showed itself.

When she opened her eyes again, she found the cold grey eyes of Halt looking back, and smirked.

"Fine, I admit it. My parents were monsters. What of it?"

She almost laughed as the doctor's face darkened, an angry red flushing his cheeks. He clenched his fists and made to approach the cage before stopping himself. Flashing a glance over his shoulder at their audience, he shook his head and smiled.

"Very good," he said, eyeing the two of them. "So, we understand one another."

7

C hris gripped the wire of his cage as Doctor Halt eyed his two prisoners. Clamping his mouth shut, he ignored the voice in his head that was screaming for answers. His whole body ached where the guards had struck him, and he was not eager to repeat the experience. The ugly thugs were grinning at him now, as though daring him to give them another chance. Instead, he bit his tongue and waited to see what came next.

His mind was still reeling, struggling to put together the pieces of his scattered memories. Images from the night flashed through his mind—the *Chead* on the television, the men in his house, his mother falling.

His throat contracted as Halt's words twisted in his mind.

Traitor.

A tremor shook him and he suppressed a sob. The sentence for treason was death. Often just an accusation was enough to doom someone. Now his mother had been taken, stolen away by the woman in the white coat.

Holding his breath, Chris struggled with his fear, his terror that she might already be gone. That he might now be alone, an orphan in a harsh, unforgiving world.

He took a great, shuddering breath. That was the least of his problems now. Whatever his mother's fate, Chris could do nothing for her, not so long as he remained trapped in this cage.

Halt's voice drew Chris's attention back to him. "Now that we have an understanding, it is time to prepare you for your time here." A thin smile spread across his lips. "Take off your clothes."

An icy hand gripped Chris's chest as Halt folded his arms. Behind the doctor, the guards edged closer, broad grins splitting their faces. A sharp intake of breath came from the other cage, but otherwise the young woman did not move.

Chris shrank away from the wire. "Why?"

Halt took a step forward. "Now, Christopher, I thought we'd moved past this. The dog does not question his master."

Clenching his fists, Chris shook his head. His eyes travelled past Halt, to the audience of doctors, lingering on the face of the woman, the doctor called Fallow. "This isn't right," he breathed.

Halt let out a long sigh and waved the guards forward. They moved towards Chris's cage with a cold proficiency. Chris hesitated, but they were already reaching the door and fumbling with the latch. Quickly, he began to unbutton his shirt, his cheeks flushing with embarrassment.

Outside, the guards paused, looking back at Halt in question. The doctor nodded curtly, and they retreated a step.

In the cage, Chris stripped off his clothing piece by piece, shivering as the icy breath of the air conditioner brushed his skin. The hairs stood up on the back of his neck as he pulled off his underwear and tossed them to the floor. Turning sideways, he bowed his head, struggling to cover himself.

Then he reached up and unclipped the chain hanging around his neck. It came away easily, the little pocket watch falling into his hand. Trembling, he flicked open the metal catch and looked at the faces of his mother and father, at their kind smiles, the life in their eyes.

Struggling to hold back tears, he closed the watch again and placed it gently, reverently, on his pile of clothes.

Standing, he felt the eyes of the gathered doctors roaming over his naked flesh, examining him, seeking out his every secret. A deep sense of helplessness rose in his chest, threatening to overwhelm him. Cheeks flushed, he stared hard at the ground, fighting to ignore the world.

"Very good, Christopher." Halt's voice was patronizing, and Chris almost choked on the shame that rose in his throat. "And you, Elizabeth?"

From the corner of his eyes, Chris caught movement in the other cage. He watched as Elizabeth approached the front of her cage. She wore a smirk on her lips, but her blue eyes flashed with unconcealed rage. She pressed herself against the wire and stared at Halt.

"Come and get me," she hissed.

Chris's eyes widened. After her earlier acquiescence, he had not expected her to resist.

Halt only gave a slow shake of his head. "Bring her," he said, gesturing to the guards.

The guards marched past him and yanked open the door to Elizabeth's cage. She retreated quickly, waiting as the first guard pushed his way inside. Then with a wild shriek, she attacked. At maybe one hundred and twenty-five pounds, she was dwarfed by the guard. But her sudden violence caught him by surprise, and he stumbled backwards into his comrade.

As the two of them went down in a heap, Elizabeth leapt for the door. She made it across the threshold before the first guard managed to stagger upright. His arm swung out, catching her by the foot, and she slammed into the concrete outside the cage. With a screech, she kicked out with her free leg, slamming her heel into the guard's face. He gave a muffled curse, but held on.

In seconds, the other guard was on his feet. He strode across to where Elizabeth still fought to free herself, reached down, and grabbed her hair in one meaty hand. The girl let out a pained cry as he lifted her up and held her off the ground. Tears streamed down her cheeks as she kicked feebly at empty air, her hands batting at his chest.

With a contemptuous flick of his arm, the guard tossed her aside. Elizabeth crashed hard into the concrete. She struggled to her knees, but a heavy boot drove down onto her back, sending her face first into the floor.

Halt walked across and knelt beside the girl, a cold smile on his snakelike lips.

"Elizabeth." Halt's voice was laced now with honey. "Be a good girl, now. You cannot begin your time here with those reminders of your old life. Remove your clothes."

Chris shuddered as Halt stood and watched the girl lift herself to her hands and knees. One trembling hand reached for the buttons of her shirt and began to pluck them open. Chris looked away, unwilling to participate in her shaming.

He glanced up a minute later as the sound of metal striking concrete rang through the room. His eyes were drawn to the object now lying on the ground between Halt and the shivering girl. The thick steel links of a chain lay between them like a snake, the silver metal shining in the fluorescent lights. For an instant, Chris wondered where it had come from, but his thoughts quickly turned to what it was.

A collar.

8

"**P**ut it on." Halt's voice slivered through the room, cold, commanding.

Elizabeth flinched away from him, but the guard's hand flashed out and caught the girl by the hair again. He shoved her back to her knees in front of the collar. A growl came from her throat as she glared up at Halt. For a second, Chris thought she would fight, but she only reached out with one trembling hand and picked up the collar.

The young woman's mouth twisted into a grimace as she held the steel linked chain in front of her. She closed her eyes, her nostrils flaring as she sucked in a breath. Chris waited, his own breath held, aware his turn would soon come.

"This is what you want, you disgusting—" Elizabeth broke off as a guard's fist sent her reeling across the floor.

Naked, she straightened on the ground, the collar still in hand. She looked at Halt, and then away again. With trembling hands, she lifted the collar to her throat. The *click* it made as it locked around her neck echoed loudly in the concrete room.

Halt smiled and clapped his hands. The guards grabbed Elizabeth by each arm and hauled her up. With a few shoves, they had her back in the cage. A pile of orange clothes was tossed in with her before the steel door swung shut. Then Halt turned on Chris, waiting naked inside his own cage.

"I suppose it's my turn then?" he asked with false bravado.

Halt stared Chris down, the grey eyes piercing him. Horror curled its way up Chris's throat as he felt his cheeks warming. His eyes drifted towards the other doctors, who still stood in silence. The guards approached his cage, one carrying a bundle of orange clothing, the other a steel linked collar identical to the one Elizabeth now wore.

"Move to the back of the cage," one of the guards ordered.

Clenching his fists, Chris stumbled back from the door as the guard flicked the latch and pushed it open. His body ached from his beating, and in the narrow space he didn't like his chances of besting the two men. He had already watched the girl attempt that approach, and fail. He would have to wait, bide his time until an opportunity arose.

Inside the cage, one guard collected his clothes, replacing them with the orange bundle. The collar was placed on top of the pile, and then the two men retreated, swinging the door shut behind them.

Chris looked at Halt, waiting for an order. When none was forthcoming, he crossed to the pile and picked up the collar. Raising an eyebrow, he tried and failed to suppress his sarcasm. "What are we, your pets?"

Halt smirked. "Would you like another lesson, Christopher?"

Letting out a long breath, Chris shook his head. He squeezed his fist, letting the cold metal of the collar dig into his flesh. His heart pounded hard in his chest, screaming a warning. Somehow, he knew if he obeyed, if he put on this collar, there would be no going back.

Dimly, he remembered a story his father had told him when he was younger. It had been almost ten years since the cancer had taken him, but he could still recall his father's voice with crystal clarity. His rough baritone drifted up from Chris's memories, as he described how the *Mahouts* in Thailand had once tamed their elephants.

The *Mahouts* placed chains around the legs of young elephants and attached them to heavy pegs in the ground. Whenever the young elephants tried to escape, the chain would contract, cutting into the elephant's leg, making it bleed. Eventually, the captive elephant would realize the futility of trying to escape.

As adults, the same chain and peg were used to restrain the giant creatures. And though by then they possessed the strength to escape the peg and chain, they never made the attempt again.

Silently, Chris wondered if that was to be his fate, if the collar in his hands would become the chain that bound him to a lifetime of servitude.

But looking at Halt, Chris knew he had no choice but to obey.

He raised the collar to his neck with deliberate slowness, as though he were approaching some great precipice. A tingle ran through him as the metal touched his skin, and a terrifying dread closed around his throat. A voice screamed for him to run, to hurl the collar away from him.

Instead, he closed his eyes and pulled the collar closed. The steel links slid across his flesh, icy to the touch, and came together with a loud *click*.

Struggling to breathe, Chris sank to his knees and fumbled for the pile of clothes. A sudden, desperate shame at his nakedness took him. He felt exposed, as though his nudity highlighted his new bondage, relegating him to nothing but an animal.

Quickly he scrambled into the bright orange uniform, and then sat with his knees pulled up to his chest. A tide of despair rose in his throat, but he pushed it down, struggling to keep a flicker of hope burning. The collar's icy grip seemed to tighten, stealing away his breath. A claustrophobic scream grew in his throat as he gasped for air.

Halt only gave a satisfied nod and stepped back from the cage.

Glancing at the other cage, Chris saw that Elizabeth had managed to pull on her own orange jumpsuit. The heavy fabric clung to her frame, and Chris couldn't help but think of what he'd glimpsed of her while naked. A bruise showed on her forehead when her clear blue eyes flickered in his direction. His cheeks warmed as she raised an eyebrow. Her wild black curls hung around her shoulders, the ends jagged and split, as though they'd been cut by a knife.

Taking a breath, the young woman pulled herself to her feet. The collar flashed around her neck, an all too vivid reminder of their new position. Her fists clenched and her lips drew back in a snarl, but otherwise she remained quiet.

Halt gave a satisfied smirk. "Very good. I'm pleased to see you're fast learners. Perhaps you will surprise me yet." Chris flinched as Halt clapped his hands again. "Now, before you are taken to your new quarters, I must warn you: I have little patience for agitators. Dissent will not be tolerated. Those collars are more than they appear. Do not attempt to remove them. Any effort to tamper with them without the correct key will have…unpleasant results."

Chris swallowed hard. A trickle of sweat ran down his neck and he tasted bile in his throat. He clenched his teeth and fought to keep himself from throwing up whatever remained in his stomach. In the opposite cage, Elizabeth showed no sign she'd heard Halt's words. She stood with her eyes closed, one arm pressed against the chain-link wall, as though that was the only thing keeping her upright.

When neither of them spoke, Halt continued: "The collars are a disciplinary tool, to rein in unruly subjects when they step out of line."

Leaning against the wall of his cage, Chris stifled a yawn, unwilling to show his fear. "And how exactly do they 'punish us'?"

The doctor glared at him, then gave a slow shake of his head. "Perhaps you are not as quick to learn as I thought."

He pulled down his sleeve, revealing a sleek black watch on his wrist, all shining metal and glass. As he tapped its surface, the screen glowed bright blue. Another tap, and a loud beep came from Chris's collar. The hairs stood up on his neck as Halt looked at him.

"Your collars are capable of delivering an electric shock of five hundred volts, at up to one hundred milliamps. They are activated remotely by these watches, which you will find all personnel within the facility are equipped with." A slow grin spread across Halt's face. "A single swipe of the screen, by any doctor or guard, and all collars within a twenty-foot radius are activated. Or an individual subject's collar may be chosen at our discretion. Perhaps you need a demonstration?"

Silently, Chris shook his head. From the corner of his eye, he saw the girl make the same gesture.

Halt watched them, his eyes aglow with a strange light. "You don't seem too enthusiastic," he laughed. "Too bad." Before anyone could move, he pressed a thumb to his watch.

Chris's collar gave a loud beep. He opened his mouth, but before any sound could escape, fingers of fire wrapped around his throat, cutting off his cry. His jaw locked as electricity surged through his body. His back arched and the strength went from his legs, sending him toppling to the concrete. A burning cramp tore into his muscles as he thrashed against the ground. The water that still pooled beneath him soaked through his clothes, but he barely noticed.

A buzzing filled his ears, but through it, he could hear Halt's voice. "This is twenty milliamps. Enough to deliver a painful shock, even freeze your motor functions. Not enough to kill—at least not when delivered for short periods of time."

Another beep sounded, and the flow of electricity ceased. Chris slumped to the ground, eyes closed, a low moan rattling in his chest. The sudden absence of pain was a sweet relief. He sucked in an eager breath, the cold air burning his throat.

As the last twitch in his muscles ceased, he cracked open his eyes and looked through the wire. He had fallen on his side and now found himself looking across at Elizabeth. She was on the ground as well, her tangled hair covering her face, her limbs splayed out across the concrete. Her forehead sported a nasty cut where she must have struck the ground.

Halt stood between the cages, the same dark grin twisting his face. His eyes found Chris's, and the smile spread.

"Welcome, Christopher and Elizabeth, to the Genome Project."

❦ 9 ❦

Angela Fallow waited until the door closed behind her before allowing the mask to crack. A sharp sob cut the air as she stumbled across the room and collapsed onto the bed. The feather-down duvet cushioned her fall, but it did nothing for the burden weighing on her soul. Burying her head in a pillow, she finally allowed the tears to flow.

What have I done?

For years she had worked in government laboratories, studying the creatures that had come to be known as the *Chead*, examining their genetic composition and identifying chromosomal alterations within their DNA. While the more superstitious citizens of the Western Allied States regarded the *Chead* as some paranormal phenomenon, she had dedicated her life to actually dissecting the mysteries of the creatures.

She had been the first to discover the link

between the *Chead* awakenings across the country. A short sequence of nucleic acids in one of her samples had put her on the trail, and within days she had confirmed her suspicions. Whether the *Chead* had woken in rural California or downtown Seattle, the same virus was present in the genome of every known *Chead.*

Porcine Endogenous Retrovirus, or PERV, was a well-known retrovirus amongst the scientific community. Since the turn of the twentieth century, the virus had been used to exchange DNA between pig and human cells. PERV was a provirus—meaning upon contraction it fully integrated into the host genome. This led to its initial use in the modification of genes within the organs of pigs, to increase their receptivity when transplanted into human subjects.

But Angela had checked the records of every *Chead,* and none had ever been a candidate for xenotransplantation.

Normally, the virus alone would have meant little. There was not a person alive whose chromosomes did not contain some viral elements. In fact, many scientists speculated that proviruses played a significant role in evolution, altering genes and alleles at a rate far faster than ordinary mutation.

However, once the link was discovered, it had not taken Angela long to piece out other discrepancies in the *Chead* chromosomes. Alongside the PERV recombinations, she identified genome markers with foundations in everything from primates to canines, eagles to rabbits. Even genes from rare animals such as the Philippine Tarsier and Cnidaria had featured in the genetic puzzle.

In the end, the evidence all pointed to a single, undeniable conclusion.

The *Chead* were no accident. Someone had created them, had designed a virus and released it into the world.

The question of *who* remained unanswered, though the government had quickly pointed the blame on that old enemy—the United States. Or at least the scattered states that remained of the once-great nation.

But the *who* was not Angela's concern. Now knowing the cause, she had applied herself to countering its spread. Fortunately, the virus did not appear to be contagious. No cases had been reported of friends or family contracting the virus from awakened *Chead*, though the government still rounded them up as a precaution.

That left the question of how the victims were infected. She suspected an external source was at work there, though if true, it was up to others to solve that puzzle.

As for those already infected, Angela had failed time and time again in the search for a cure. Ordinary viruses incorporated themselves into the host DNA, much as the *Chead* virus had done. However, the similarities ended there. Symptoms of an ordinary viral infection arose when a virus began self-replication, eventually leading to cell rupture and the spread of virons to other cells. Sickness showed as human cells were hijacked by the virons and used for further self-replication.

Instead of following this route, the *Chead* virus remained latent within its host's DNA. In fact, it was almost perfectly incorporated into the human chromosome. The symptoms exhibited by the *Chead* were the result of gene expression in the cells themselves—only appearing once those genes activated. Similar to how many babies had blue eyes at birth, until their genes for brown eyes began to express.

In other words, the virus was a part of the *Chead* now, and no matter how Angela tried to approach the problem, she could find no possibility for a cure.

Upon learning of her discovery, the government had made the call to take Angela's research in a new direction. They had transferred her here to work with other doctors on the Genome Project – their own answer to the spread of the *Chead*.

A new virus was being shaped, one of such complexity and ingenious, Angela could not help but wonder how long it had been in development. Once perfected, it would change the world forever. Now, with Angela's help, they were close to a breakthrough. Initial trials on bovine subjects had proven successful, but Halt and his government overseers wanted more. They were desperate for an answer, for a beacon of hope to hold up to the people. Even the usually ice-cold Halt had appeared flustered in recent weeks, and she sensed that far more than her career rested on what happened over the next few weeks and months.

Shivering, Angela wrapped her arms tightly around herself. Not for the first time, she wondered what her life would have been like had she taken a different path. Deep in her soul, she still longed for the wild open space of the countryside, the endless stars and unmarked horizons. Her family's ranch had been remote, far from the bustling hives of the cities —though of course, it had not really been *theirs*. They worked the land, harvested the crops, while the landowner in the city took the profits.

As a young girl, she had resented that fact, and the limitations of rural life. So she had studied and schemed, and won a place in a scholarship program in Los Angeles. She had grasped the opportunity with both hands, and run off to find her place in the big wide world.

Funny how things changed, with thirty-five years' worth of wisdom.

The world was a wild place, but in the city, life was far less forgiving than in the country.

Angela shuddered as she heard again the awful screams, watched as the girl writhed on the floor of the cage. In the silence of her mind, Angela imagined the girl's crystal blue eyes seeking her out, begging for help.

Another sob tore from Angela's throat. Those eyes, that face; they were so like her own. In those youthful features, she saw her past, saw the girl she had once been reflected back.

What have I done?

The question came again, persistent. She had never thought it would come to this. When Halt had told her their plan to gather candidates for human trials, it had seemed simple. Family members convicted of treason were destined to suffer the same fate as the accused. So why not make use of those lives?

Young, healthy candidates were needed for the trials to maximize the chances of success. The children of traitors seemed the perfect answer to their needs.

Only now that she faced the reality of that decision, it was more awful than she could ever have imagined. Halt might see the children as a means to an end, but Angela could not look past their humanity. Halt was a monster, seeming to delight in the breaking of each new candidate, but for Angela, the guilt ate at her soul.

She heard again the *thud* of fists on flesh. Her stomach swirled and it was all she could do not to throw up.

"What have I done?" she whispered.

The plain walls of her private quarters offered no answers, only their silent judgement. This was her life, this little white room, the empty double bed, the white dresser and coatrack beside the door. Her woolen fleece hung on the rack, untouched for weeks now.

Staring at it, Angela was taken by an impulse to escape, to leave this place and walk out into the wilderness beyond the facility's walls. She stood and tore the coat from its rack. Swinging it around her shoulders, she fastened the buttons and pushed open the door.

The corridor outside ran left and right. Left led deeper into the facility, where her laboratory and the prison cells waited. She turned right, moving past the closed doors of the staff living quarters. It was well past midnight, and everyone else would have retired long ago. Only the night guards would be awake.

It only took a few minutes to reach the outer door —a fire exit, but from past excursions she knew there was no alarm attached. The heavy steel door watched her approach, unmoved by her sorrow. Placing her shoulder to it, she gave a hard shove and pulled at the latch.

The sharp screech of unoiled hinges echoed down the corridor, followed by a blast of cold wind.

Clenching her teeth, Angela pushed it wider and slipped out into the darkness. She pulled her coat tighter as a tendril of ice slid down her back, and listened as the door clicked shut behind her. She wasn't concerned—there were no locks on the outer doors. Out here, break-ins were the least of their worries.

Beyond the light streaming from the facility, night beckoned. Angela sucked in a long breath of mountain air and looked up at the sky. A thousand pinpricks of light dotted the darkness, the full scope of the Milky Way laid bare before her. The pale sliver of a crescent moon cast dim shadows across the rocky ground, where a thin layer of snow dotted the stones.

Shivering, Angela watched her breath mist in the freezing air. It was eerie, staring out into the absolute black. Other than the stars, no light showed beyond the facility. They were far from civilization here, miles into the mountains, as remote as one could be within the Western Allied States.

Staring at the stars, Angela could almost imagine herself a child again. A desperate yearning rose within her, to return to the simplicity of that life, to the warmth of her family ranch.

She sucked in another breath, watching the darkness, imagining the long curves of the hidden mountains. The first snow had arrived a few days ago, heralding the onset of winter. Climatologists were predicting a strong *El Niño* though, meaning a mild winter.

Standing there in the darkness, with the icy wind

biting at her skin, Angela could not help but disagree. This winter would be long and savage, and few at the facility would survive it. Only the strongest would endure.

She hoped the candidates would prove up to the challenge. They had only one chance, one opportunity. Fail now, and the government would end it all.

Bowing her head, Angela turned back to the fire door. She pushed it open and returned to the warm light of the corridor. Once inside, she leaned against the door and slid to the floor.

Just a little longer. She clung desperately to the thought.

Just a little longer, and she could rest, could put this all behind her.

Just a little longer, and she would save the world.

❧ 10 ❧

C*lang.*

Liz flinched as the cell door slammed shut behind her, the harsh sound slashing through her self-control. She clenched her fists, fighting to stop the trembling in her body. Every fiber of her being screamed for her to run, to hide, but she sucked in a breath instead, calming her nerves. Cold steel pressed against her throat, a constant reminder of her captivity.

A sharp pain came from her palms as her nails dug into flesh. With a great effort, she unclenched her fists. The breath caught in her throat, but she swallowed and sucked in another, refusing to give in to her panic. The thick threads of the orange uniform rubbed her skin uncomfortably, though in truth its quality was better than anything she'd scavenged in the past two years.

Liz cast her eyes over her new home. The plain concrete walls matched what she'd glimpsed of the rest of the facility on the short trip from cage to prison cell. The journey had taken less than five minutes, a quick march down long corridors, past open doors and strange rooms filled with glass tubes and steel contraptions. Some she recognized from her boarding school: beakers and test tubes and other things she'd forgotten the names of. But most were beyond her understanding—plastic boxes that hummed and whirred, steel cubes of unknown purpose, containers filled with a strange, gel-like substance.

The guards had ushered them past each room with quick efficiency, leaving no time for questions. Only once had Liz paused, when they'd passed a room apparently used as a canteen. The smell of coffee and burnt toast wafted out, and she'd seen a dozen people sitting around a table, talking quietly. Before Liz could speak, a guard had jabbed the butt of his rifle into the small of her back.

A little gasp had burst from her lips, and several people inside had glanced her way. Several had raised their eyebrows at the sight of her, but a moment later they returned to their conversations. Seeing their indifference, Liz had felt the last of her courage curdle.

From there they'd been led through a thick iron door, into the grim corridor of a prison block. Faces lined the cells to either side of them as they marched past. Wide eyes stared out, their owners no more than children, ranging from around thirteen to twenty years of age.

Now Liz stood in a tiny concrete cell, the iron bars at her back locking her in, sealing her off from the outside world. Two sets of bunk beds had been pushed against the walls on her left and right, while at the rear a toilet and sink were bolted into the floor. Curtains dangled down beside the toilet, presumably to offer some small semblance of privacy.

And between the bunks stood her new roommates.

The boy and girl stared back at Liz and Christopher. The boy stood well over six feet, his muscled shoulders and arms dwarfing the girl beside him. His skin was the dark hue of a Native American, except where a scar stretched down his right arm. Black hair hung around his razor-sharp face, and hawkish brown eyes studied her with detached curiosity.

The girl beside him could not have been a starker contrast. Her pale skin practically shone in the overhead lights, unmarked by so much as a freckle, and at around five foot three, she barely came up to the boy's chest. She stood with arms folded, her posture defensive, though with her thin frame Liz doubted she could fend off a toddler. Long hair hung down to her waist, the scarlet locks well-trimmed but unwashed. Had it not been for that, Liz might have thought she'd just finished a photoshoot.

But on closer inspection, Liz noticed the faint marks of bruises on her arms, the traces of purple on her cheeks, and dark circles beneath her tawny yellow eyes. Cuts and old scars marked her knuckles, and several of her once-long nails were broken.

Maybe not so harmless after all, Liz mused.

The boy from the cages, Christopher, stood beside her, completing their party of four. Although it wasn't much of a party. So far they'd gone a full minute without speaking.

Outside, the last thud of boots ceased, and the crash of the outer doors closing heralded the departure of their escort.

Between the bunks, the boy came to life. "Welcome to hell." He spoke with a northern accent as he offered a hand. "I'm Sam, I'll be your captain today. Ashley here will be your hostess."

Beside him, Ashley rolled her eyes but did not speak.

Liz winced as she recognized the urban twang. With her pale skin, it was obvious the girl had never spent any time in the sun tending to crops or livestock, but Liz had at least hoped she might share a kinship with the boy. A lonely sorrow rose within her as she wrapped her arms around herself. It seemed not only was she to be locked away, but her roommates were going to be a bunch of kids straight out of prep school.

"Ah…" Christopher sounded confused by their new roommate's banter. "My name's Chris, and ah…this is Elizabeth, I guess."

Liz heard the shuffling of feet, no doubt the sound of the two shaking hands. Shivering, she blinked back the sudden tears that sprang to her eyes, determined to keep her weakness to herself. Her head throbbed where the guards had struck her, and a dull ache came from the small of her back.

The tremor came again, the cold air of the room eating at her resistance. She looked up to find three sets of eyes studying her. A frown creased Sam's forehead and his mouth opened, as though to ask a question, but she turned away before he could speak. A sudden yearning to be alone took her, a need for the peaceful quiet of open fields and forests. The concrete walls seemed to be closing on her, the still air suffocating.

Her eyes found the beds, taking in the unmade sheets on the bottom two. The sheets of the top bunks were pulled tight, untouched by sleep.

Without a word, she stumbled past Sam and Ashley and grasped at the ladder. Arms shaking, she pulled herself up and rolled onto the hard mattress of her new bed.

"She's a friendly one," Sam's voice carried up to her, but Liz only closed her eyes, and willed away the sounds. Her breath came in ragged gasps as she tried to still her racing heart.

"She's just scared," was Chris's uncertain reply.

You're wrong, she thought.

She was angry, horrified, frustrated, and more than anything in the world she just wanted to curl up in a corner and cry. But instead, she found herself trapped in a tiny cell with three teenagers from the city—two young men and a woman who would never understand her, her past.

"She should be," said Sam, his voice taking on a bitter tone, "you two haven't even seen the worst of it yet."

Sam's voice put Liz on edge, dragging her back from the peace she sought, but she kept her mouth shut. Scuffling came from below as the three moved, then her bunk shifted as someone sat on the bed underneath her. Cracking open one eye, Liz saw the two boys still standing, and guessed Ashley had retreated to her bed.

"I don't plan on sticking around to find out," Chris spoke in a hoarse whisper. "I have to get out of here."

Laughter followed his statement. "Don't we all, kid," Sam replied jokingly, "but it's kind of a one-way ticket."

"I don't care." Chris's voice was sharp with anger. "Fallow...that woman, she took my mother. I can't, I can't let anything happen to her."

"Tough luck, kid. Wherever she is, she's going to have to cope without you. The only way out of here is in a body bag. Just be glad it wasn't our pal Doctor Halt who grabbed her—although I'm sure he could arrange a reunion if you asked him nicely."

Below, Chris swore. "How can you joke?" he snarled, his voice rising. "Don't you understand? There's been some mistake. My mother hasn't done anything wrong. Her father died in the American War; she would never betray the WAS—"

"And you think we're any different?" the larger boy snapped, the humor falling from his voice. "You think we all conspired against the government? Don't be a fool. There's no going back, no changing things now. Not for any of us."

Silence fell over the cell. A grin tugged at Liz's lips as she embraced the quiet, taking the opportunity to calm her roiling thoughts. The lights were bright overhead, burning through her eyelids, but at least the assault on her ears had ceased. Thinking of the other three, she felt a pang of empathy, a sadness for their loss. They were orphans now too, same as her.

Perhaps she was not so alone, after all.

"It doesn't matter." Chris's voice came as a whisper now. "I'll find a way."

Sam chuckled. "You and what army? Even if you could remove that collar, if you could break out of this cell, where would you go? Who would help you,

Chris? You're the son of a traitor, a fugitive without rights."

A rustling came from below, followed by a yelp. Liz's eyes widened as Chris pushed Sam up against the wall.

"She's not a traitor," Chris retorted, "and like I said, it doesn't matter. I'm not going to sit here and give up. I'm not going to let them win."

Sam's eyes hardened and he reached up with deliberate slowness to remove Chris's hands from his shirt.

"Listen, *kid.*" His voice was threatening now. "You still don't get it, do you? We mean *nothing* to these people. You'll find that out tomorrow, how *little* your life means. They'll kill you the second you cross them."

"Let them try," Chris snapped.

Sam's face darkened, and then it was his turn to grab Chris by the shirt. Without apparent effort, he lifted Chris off the ground, leaving the smaller boy kicking feebly at empty air.

"Believe me, I couldn't care less if you get yourself killed," Sam snapped, "but since we're trapped in here together, chances are, your stupidity will get us *all* executed—"

Sam broke off as Chris twisted in his grasp and drove a foot into the larger boy's stomach. Air exploded between Sam's teeth as he staggered backwards, dropping Chris unceremoniously. Chris landed lightly on his feet and straightened, eyeing Sam from across the cell.

Liz raised an eyebrow as the two faced off against each other.

"*Enough!*" A girl's sharp voice cut the air.

The two boys jumped as Ashley strode forward with a catlike grace to stand between them. She turned to Sam and placed a hand on his chest. Her eyes flickered from him to Chris, a gentle smile warming her face.

"Enough," she said again, softly this time. Even so, there was strength to her words.

Liz watched with surprise as Sam's shoulders slumped, his tension fleeing at Ashley's touch. Chris stared, his eyes hesitant, before lowering his fists. The smile still on her lips, Ashley gave a quick nod.

"We can't fight amongst ourselves," she chided, like a teacher reprimanding her students. "Sam, you know that better than anyone. We need each other."

She turned towards Chris then, her eyes soft. "Chris, I know you're afraid, that you're terrified for your mother. I know it's awful, that you're confused. But you must calm yourself. Your mother would not want you to throw your life away."

Liz blinked, shocked by the calm manner with which Ashley had taken control of the situation. Despite her reservations, she found herself warming to the girl.

Below, Ashley turned back to Sam. "Sam, you

can't hide behind that charade. Not from me." She paused, her tawny eyes watching him. "Not after everything we've been through."

Sam bowed his head. "You caught me, as usual," he said with a shrug, before throwing himself down on his bed. "I still don't want him getting us all killed, though!"

Ashley nodded. Her eyes swept the room, lingering for a second as they caught Liz watching her, before turning to Chris. She approached him and placed a hand on his shoulder.

"You are not alone, Chris," she whispered. "Wherever you came from before, we are in this together now. We're family, you and I. All of us." Ashley's voice shook as she spoke. "And you're right. We can't just give up. We *will* find a way out of here, together. Whoever these people are, they are only human. They're not perfect. Eventually they'll make a mistake, leave some hole in their defenses. And when they do, we'll be ready for them; we'll take our chance."

Liz's heart lurched as the yellow eyes flickered back to her. "That goes for you too, Elizabeth."

Warmth spread to Liz's cheeks as the other girl watched her. She nodded slowly, struggling to cover her embarrassment. Listening to Ashley's words, she could almost feel a flicker of hope stir inside her. Maybe she wasn't alone after all. Whatever their differences, Ashley was right. They were in this together now.

Sitting up, Liz placed her hands on the bed and propelled herself off the side. She landed lightly, her bare feet slapping against the concrete, and straightened in front of Ashley. A smile, genuine now, tugged at her lips, but she tried to maintain a stoic expression. She didn't want to get too far ahead of herself —they were still from the city, after all.

Liz took a deep breath and offered Ashley her hand.

"You can call me Liz."

II

TRYOUTS

Chris exhaled hard as he rounded the final bend in the track, his lungs burning with the exertion. Pain tore through his calves and his stomach gave a sickening lurch, but he pressed on. The dusty track gripped easily beneath his bare feet, propelling him on towards the finish line. From behind came the ragged breathing of the others, some hot on his heels, others a long way back.

Allowing himself a smile, Chris glanced to the side, and almost tripped when he saw Liz draw alongside him. The black-haired girl had her head down, eyes fixed to the track, and was picking up the pace. Panting hard, Chris followed suit, and side by side, they raced down the final straight.

Over the last few yards, Chris's feet barely touched the ground. Shadows swirled at the edges of his vision, exhaustion threatening. Through the darkness, he glimpsed Liz pulling ahead, saw her wild grin as she crossed the line a millisecond before him.

Drawing to a stop beside her, Chris shook his head, his mouth unable to form words. Bending in two, he sucked in a mouthful of air. He felt lightheaded, his lungs aflame. It took him a full minute to catch his breath. By then the others had finished up the race.

Lowering himself to the ground, Chris blinked sweat from his eyes. Using one large orange sleeve, he wiped his forehead clear and shook his head at Liz.

"You're fast," he croaked.

It was the second day since their awakening, and the two of them had still barely spoken. Despite her reluctant greeting in the cell, Liz remained withdrawn.

The young woman only shrugged. Two blue eyes glanced down, then away. "It's the air," she breathed. "We're in the mountains—I can taste it. You're probably not used to the altitude."

Chris nodded, stars still dancing across his vision. A groan built in his throat as he saw Liz straighten, but he pushed it down and lifted himself to his feet. Ignoring the ache in his muscles, they joined the others.

Sam and Ashley stood with their hands on their hips, looking like they'd barely broken a sweat. Chris cursed himself for exerting so much energy. Who knew what else the day had in store for them?

Yesterday, he and Liz had been taken into a laboratory and put through a series of tests. The doctors had worked with a cool efficiency, asking questions, giving instructions, taking measurements, all the while steadfastly refusing to engage with their captives. Behind the doctors, the guards had been colder still, their hard eyes following the prisoners' every movement.

The tests had been simple enough, little more than a thorough examination by the local GP. But now, it seemed, the easy part was over. That morning they had been roused in the early hours by a shrieking alarm and the sudden brilliance of overhead lights. For a few seconds Chris had tried to resist, exhausted after a long night spent tossing and turning, unable to sleep. But Sam and Ashley had been insistent, dragging them from their beds to stand for inspection.

Within minutes, the guards had marched past. A doctor had accompanied them, pausing outside each cell to make notes on his electronic tablet. Chris had shivered as the man's eyes fell on him. There was a mindless, mechanical way in which he took the roster, as though this was no more than an inventory check at the grocery store.

When the doctor had departed, the guards returned with a trolley. The hallway had rung with the sound of bowls sliding through metal grates. Chris had stared for a long while at the oatmeal congealing in his bowl before the rumbling of his stomach won him over. Resigning himself, he'd taken up his spoon and eaten all he could.

Then their escort of doctors and guards had arrived, taking them from the quiet of their cell and marching them through the facility to this field—if it could be called that. The open space was the size of a football field, but there was not a blade of grass in sight.

Instead, a fine dust covered the ground, spreading out across the oval like snow. A running track ran around its circumference, edged by tall, imposing walls that hemmed them in on all sides. The cold grey concrete stretched up almost thirty feet, interspersed with the metal railings of observation decks. A dozen guards looked down on them, rifles held in ready arms. The only building was a stone tower that rose some forty feet from the center of the field.

Overhead, the sun beat down from a cloudless blue sky. The world outside was hidden by the walls, and whether Liz's mountains existed beyond remained a mystery.

Other than the doctors and their escort of guards, the field was empty. The doctors had made quick notes on their ever-present tablets, before nodding to the guards. Orders had been barked, and the four of them had set off running.

Now they stood together in a little circle, panting softly as they waited for the next command. The doctors hovered nearby, their attention fixed on their tablets, talking quietly amongst themselves. The guards stood nearby, their dark eyes fixed on the prisoners.

Beyond the little group of overseers, a red light started to flash above the door they'd entered through. A buzzer sounded, short and sharp. The guards straightened, turning to face the entrance as the door gave a loud *click* and swung inwards.

Another group of doctors entered, followed by four prisoners in matching orange uniforms. Chris scanned the faces of the doctors, searching for Fallow, but there was no sign of her. His shoulders slumped and he clenched his fists, struggling to contain his disappointment. The woman was his only remaining link to his mother, but Fallow had been conspicuously absent since their initiation.

As the group walked towards them, Chris sensed movement beside him. Glancing at the others, he was surprised to see Sam's face harden, the easy smile slipping from his lips. The older boy grasped Ashley by the wrist, nodding in the direction of the newcomers. Ashley's face paled and she stumbled sideways before Sam caught her.

"What?" Chris hissed.

The two glanced at one another and then shook their heads. "Nothing," Sam muttered.

The new group of inmates reached them before Chris could ask anything more. They hovered a few paces away, three boys and a girl, studying Chris and the others with suspicion. Chris stared back, wondering at the reaction of Sam and Ashley.

Clearing his throat, one of the doctors stepped between the two groups. He glanced at his tablet, then left and right. "Ashley and Samuel. Richard and Jasmine. You have already qualified for the next round of trials. You're here to ensure your health does not deteriorate."

Chris watched a flicker of discomfort cross the faces of a boy and girl in the opposite group, and guessed they were the ones the man was addressing. Richard sported short blond hair and angry green eyes that did not waver from Ashley and Sam. He was almost a foot shorter than Sam, but more than matched the larger boy for muscle. He kept his arms crossed tight, his stocky shoulders hunched, and a scowl fixed on his face.

The girl, who he guessed was Jasmine, stood head to head with Richard, a matching glare on her lips. Her hair floated in the breeze, the black locks brushing across her face. The skin around her brown eyes pinched as she turned towards Chris and caught him staring. Air hissed between her teeth as she raised one eyebrow.

Chris quickly looked away, his heart beginning to race. The doctor standing between them had turned his attention back to them.

"Elizabeth, Christopher, today we will test your fitness and athleticism, to assess your suitability for the next stage of the program. William and Joshua will be joining you. I suggest you get acquainted."

Chris's gaze drifted to the other two boys, and found them staring back. Their eyes did not hold the same animosity as Jasmine's and Richard's, just a wary distrust. The one on the left was a scrawny stickman of a figure, his long arms and legs little more than bone. Sharp cheekbones stood out on his face, and his jade-green eyes held more than a hint of fear. The other was larger, his arms well-muscled, but he did not match Richard or Sam for sheer bulk. He stood several inches above Chris's five-foot-eleven, and had long blond hair that hung down around his shoulders.

Seeing neither of the two were about to introduce themselves, Chris made to step towards them, but Sam's hand flashed out, catching him by the shoulder. Chris glanced at the larger boy and raised an eyebrow, but Sam only shook his head. Settling back into line, Chris glanced at Liz and saw his own confusion reflected in her eyes. Ashley's hand was clenched around Liz's wrist, holding her back.

The doctor glanced between the two groups, and with a shrug, pressed on. "Very well." He cleared his throat. "All of you, line up." He paused as the eight of them moved hesitantly to stand in one line, and then nodded. "Today—"

The doctor broke off as the buzzer by the entrance sounded again. As one, the group turned towards the door. Chris shuddered as he saw Doctor Halt striding towards them.

❦ 12 ❦

Doctor Halt's arms swung casually at his sides, as though this were no more than a Sunday stroll for him. A smile played across his thin lips. He drew to a stop alongside the doctor that had been addressing them.

"Doctor Radly," he said, his voice like honey. "How goes training day?"

"...Good," Radly answered with hesitation. He was obviously surprised to see Halt. "How can I help you, sir?"

Soft laughter whispered from Halt's lips. "I thought I might assist." His eyes slid over the group of prisoners. "We need to advance our schedule—the Director is demanding results."

Radly bit his lips, eyeing Chris and the others uncertainly. "We have four candidates ready in this unit. We still need time to assess the remaining four. Most of the other units are on a similar progression."

Shaking his head, Halt strode down the line of prisoners. When Halt had passed, Chris risked a glance at the others. Sam and Ashley stared straight ahead, steadfastly ignoring the presence of Richard and Jasmine beside them. On Chris's other side, Liz stood with her arms folded, while beyond the two newcomers wore uncertain frowns.

The crunch of gravel warned Chris of Halt's return, and he quickly faced straight ahead again. The man stared hard at Chris as he passed, then moved on to Liz. The thud of his boots continued down the line as he went on to examine Joshua and William, before returning once again.

Scowling, Halt returned to Doctor Radly. He pointed at Liz, then to the lanky boy from the other group. "Those two." He scowled. "Pitiful creatures if ever I saw them. They won't last long."

Radly opened his mouth, then closed it. Glancing at his e-tablet, he shook his head and looked back at Halt. "Sir, we have a framework in place…" He trailed off beneath Halt's withering stare.

Silence fell across the group of doctors. Chris glanced sideways at Liz, his heart beating hard against his chest. The girl stood staring straight ahead, her brow creased, fists clenched at her side. Though she did not move an inch, Chris could sense the tension building in her tiny frame, like a cat preparing to spring.

"Well, let's see," came Halt's voice again. A second later he strode past Chris and stopped in front of Liz. "Elizabeth Flores." He looked her up and down, but Liz did nothing to acknowledge his presence. Nodding, Halt moved onto his next victim. "William Beth." He smirked. "A sorry excuse for a man."

A tremor went through the boy as he stepped back and raised his hands. "Please, sir, please, I'll do whatever you say."

Halt advanced, and the boy stumbled backwards. His feet slipped in the dust and he crashed to the ground. Towering over him, Halt sneered. "Pathetic," he spat. "Get up."

William nodded. He scrambled to his feet, eyes wide with terror. "Please——"

His plea was cut short as Halt's hand flashed out and caught him by the throat. Without apparent effort, the doctor hoisted the boy into the air. William gave a half-choked scream, his face paling. His hands batted at Halt's arm, his legs kicking feebly in the air, but Halt did not waver. He watched with cold grey eyes as the boy's struggles slowly grew weaker.

Chris watched in horror, his mouth open in a silent scream. A voice in his head shouted for him to help the boy, but as he shifted, an iron hand caught him by the wrist. He glanced back, opening his mouth to argue, but the words died on his lips. There was a cold despair in Sam's eyes, a haggard look to his face. Slowly, he shook his head.

Turning back, Chris watched as Halt tossed William aside. A low groan came from the boy as he landed, his legs collapsing beneath him. Dust billowed as he fell. Gasping for breath, he struggled to his hands and knees and tried to crawl away.

Halt followed at a casual stroll. Without taking his eyes from the boy, he spoke. "You are all here by my will. But I have no use for the weak." Apparently losing patience with his victim, he drove his boot into the small of the boy's back. William collapsed face-first into the ground.

Lifting his foot, Halt stared down at the boy. "Get up."

Arms shaking, William managed to lift himself to his hands and knees. His face beet-red, he looked up at Halt. Swaying where he crouched, a tremor shook him, but he made no move to stand.

"Wretched specimen," Halt growled. "Well, if won't get off your hands and knees, it'll have to be pushups."

A confused look came over the boy's face. "Push…pushups?"

"Yes." Halt took a step closer, his face darkening. "This is your last chance to prove yourself."

William shook his head. "I…what?"

"*Now!*" Halt glanced at the other doctors, who

stood unmoving, their eyes on the trembling prisoner. "Radly, you can call the count."

At Halt's feet, a sharp sob came from William. Slowly, he placed his hands on the ground and spread his legs. As Radly shouted out each number, William lowered himself to within an inch of the ground and then straightened his arms again.

Chris and the others watched on as Radly continued to count. Beside him, Liz's expression was unreadable, though there was a slight sheen to her eyes.

As Radly reached fifteen, William's arms began to tremble. His breath came in ragged gasps and his face flushed red. A shudder ran through his bony body, and with a sob he collapsed to the ground. A triumphant grin spread across Halt's face.

"Sixteen," Radly repeated the call.

"Please," William coughed, lying with limbs splayed across the ground, "please, please I can't!"

"Keep going," Halt snarled.

He tried, no one could take that from him. Veins bulging in his forehead, teeth clenched, arms shaking with the effort, the boy managed half a pushup before he collapsed again. This time he didn't bother to beg, but just lay staring up at Halt, a haunted look in his eyes.

Halt glanced at Chris and the others. "In case you were wondering, this is what 'weakness' looks like." His cold eyes still on them, Halt reached down and tapped the sleek black glass of his watch.

Chris flinched as an awful scream came from the boy. He stumbled backwards as William started to thrash, half-gasped screams clawing their way up from his throat. Eyes wide and staring, William's head slammed back against the ground. His fingers bent, scrambling at the steel collar around his neck, even as another convulsion tore through him.

Panic gripped Chris and he stepped towards the boy. Sam's iron grasp stopped him again, pulling him back. Chris swore, struggling to break free, unable to stand by and watch the torture any longer. But Sam stood unyielding, though his eyes never left the convulsing boy. Ashley stood as still as a statue, her eyes fixed on William, her face expressionless. Her scarlet hair blew across her face, but she did not so much as raise a hand to brush it away.

The fight went from Chris in a rush.

"Such a shame, to see our people come to this," Halt said, his words slithering through the air. "Once upon a time we were proud, strong. Our forefathers marched to war with joy in their hearts and sent the cowards of the United States scurrying. Even then they did not stop. They followed the enemy back to their holes, and left a smoking crater in the heart of their so-called democracy."

Chris gritted his teeth. William's struggles were

weakening, his eyes sliding closed. Agony contorted his features, twisting his face into an awful scowl.

And still Halt spoke. "How your ancestors would turn in their graves to know of your treachery, of your betrayal of the nation they fought to create."

Chris forced his eyes closed. The hand on his shoulder gave a gentle squeeze, but Sam stayed silent. Through the strangled screams, Halt's words dug their way into Chris's consciousness. The wrinkled, smiling face of his grandmother drifted through his mind. He remembered her telling him how her husband, Chris's grandfather, had fought and died in the American War.

In 2020, horrified at the chaos engulfing their nation, a conglomerate of Washington, Oregon and California had unilaterally ceded from the United States. Arizona and New Mexico had quickly joined them, as support poured in from Canada and Mexico.

War was quick to follow, and a decade of conflict had brought both sides to their knees. Only one last, desperate gamble by the Western Allied States had assured their victory. In one decisive nuclear strike, Washington, DC was left in ruins, the leadership of the United States decimated in a single day. The union had crumbled then, leaving a scattering of independent states who either sued for peace, or were overrun.

Many argued the values of both nations had

been lost the day Washington DC fell. The Western Allied States had been left tainted, their ideals corrupted by that one act of nuclear evil. Watching Halt torture the helpless boy, Chris could not help but agree.

"Perhaps some of you will prove worthy, might one day live up to the memories of your ancestors."

Arms folded, Halt stared down at the boy. The light on William's collar still flashed red, though his twitching had slowed to little jerks of his arms and legs. He let out a long sigh. "I will give the boy this, he does not die easily." He reached for his watch.

"*Halt.*" Halt froze as a woman's voice carried across the dirt field.

The group turned as one, staring as Doctor Fallow strode through the doorway. Chris blinked. So engrossed had he been in William and Halt, he had not heard the buzz of her entrance. Now, as she marched across the dusty ground, Fallow tapped the watch on her wrist. Beside Halt, William's convulsions came to a sudden stop.

For a moment, Chris thought the boy had finally succumbed to the collar. Then a low groan came from his twisted body, and Chris let out a sigh of relief.

Fallow drew to a stop in front of Halt, her eyes flashing with anger. "What the *hell* do you think you're doing?" she growled.

❧ 13 ❧

"**W**hat the *hell* do you think you're doing?" Angela Fallow growled, her heart pounding as Halt turned to face her.

"My job." Halt's eyes flashed, and Angela took an involuntary step backwards.

Silently cursing her weakness, Angela drew herself up. "Your job is to oversee this facility, Halt. Mine is to ensure we have the right candidates for the project." Her eyes flickered to the boy at Halt's feet, and her stomach swirled.

He lay unconscious on the ground, an angry red rash spreading out from beneath the collar at his throat. He gave the odd twitch as his muscles spasmed, but otherwise he was still, the only sign of life the dull rattling of his breath. It looked like she had arrived just in time. One of the doctors had alerted her to Halt's interference with their e-tablet, but she had been on the other side of the facility.

Halt took a step towards her, his fists clenched. "Need I remind you, Fallow, you answer to me."

This time Angela did not back down. She lifted her head, facing the taller doctor. "Not in this, Halt. The trials are *mine* to oversee. The framework was designed by all of us; we *all* agreed to follow it while vetting the candidates." She twisted her lips. "However distasteful some of us may consider the methods."

Taking another step, Halt towered over her. His eyes burned, and for a long moment, he did not speak. She stared him down, unwilling to break, to give in. Halt had gone too far, stepped a mile past the lines of human decency. Whoever their prisoners were, they did not deserve to be treated like this.

The breath went from Halt in a rush. He waved a hand and turned away. "Very well, Fallow." He said the words lightly, but she did not miss the warning beneath them. He glanced at the watching doctors. "We shall do things your way. But we cannot wait. I want the next round of trials started tomorrow. The final batch of candidates are needed by the week's end."

Swallowing, Angela glanced at her coworkers. They hovered in a group, a mixture of fear and disdain in their eyes. She knew some would support her, eager to do things by the book. But others she was not so sure about. They were more willing to take risks, to press on without concern for the candidates brought to the facility. Or they were just plain terrified of Halt.

Angela could not blame them for their fear. She had once regarded the man with respect, but since his elevation to head doctor, he had revealed a darker side. Doctors who crossed him were terminated without cause, safety procedures had been cut, and with the subjects, there were no limits to his cruelty.

She eyed him now, silently calculating the population of subjects still to be vetted. There were two hundred prisoners in the facility, with roughly half of them already processed. That left a hundred candidates still to vet—of which fifty would hopefully survive to begin the experiment. It would take a mammoth effort to have them ready by the end of the week.

And that wasn't even accounting for the final touches she needed to make on the virus.

"A week's not enough time," she said.

Halt shrugged. "I'm sorry, Fallow, that's out of my hands. The Director wants results. The population is growing restless. They want answers, protection, and if the government doesn't provide them…" He trailed off.

Angela eyes travelled over the prisoners in their orange jumpsuits. She shivered as she caught the boy from San Francisco watching at her. She quickly looked away again, seeing the accusation written across his face, hearing again the screams of his mother as they took her.

Biting her lip, Angela faced Halt. "We'll have to skip the resting period. It may result in a sub-optimal outcome."

Halt waved a hand. He was already moving towards the doorway, leaving his victim lying face-down in the dust. "You will find a solution, Fallow." Their eyes met. "I know you will."

Angela's breath caught in her throat, but she held his gaze until he turned away. She shuddered as he disappeared through the iron doors, the fight falling from her like water. A muffled groan slipped from her lips, but she bit it back and turned towards the gathered doctors.

They stared back at her, awaiting instruction.

Angela straightened. "Okay, you heard Halt. We need to get these candidates classified. You know the drill." She clapped her hands and smiled as the other doctors broke from their silent reverie.

One by one, they moved away, each taking one of the orange-garbed candidates with them. Doctor Radly took the boy, Christopher, by the arm, but the boy's eyes were fixed in her direction. Looking away, Angela studied a cloud overhead. Her mind drifted, remembering again the way Margaret Sanders had fought. The woman had downed a highly-trained Marine—had almost killed him, in fact.

A mother's love.

Idly, she remembered her own mother, the way she had fussed over their little family. Despite the wide expanse of the property on which they'd lived, they had always struggled, making do with what rations the landowner left for them. But her mother had suffered their poverty with good grace, stewing rabbit bones and baking hard bread in the coal oven.

She imagined that Margaret Sanders possessed a similar resolve, a determination to do whatever it took to protect her family.

So why, then, had she been so foolish? Her treason had doomed herself and her son. Only by the grace of the government had Chris not been tossed into an interrogation cell alongside her. She shuddered, thinking of those dark places, imagining the woman's pretty face bruised and beaten.

Out on the field, Chris was running as he had been instructed, while Doctor Radly studied readings on his tablet. The collars transmitted a constant stream of data: heartbeat, blood pressure, oxygen levels, and a range of other readings. That information would be used to rank them later.

Watching the candidates, Angela turned her thoughts to what lay ahead. She shuddered as a darkness settled on her soul. Again, she reminded herself what was at stake, of the necessity of these trials. Again, she could not quite convince herself.

❧ 14 ❧

Chris drew in a long breath as he studied the wall before him, and tried to quell the trembling in his knees. The sound of the other candidates training echoed from all around him, but where he stood, Chris was alone. The stone tower in the center of the field stretched some forty feet above him, its surface smooth but for a series of climbing holds leading to the top.

"What are you waiting for?" The doctor assigned to Chris interrupted his thoughts. "Get on with it. Climb."

Swallowing, Chris flicked the man a glance. The collar seemed to tighten around his throat as he glimpsed the watch on his captors wrist, and shuddering Chris returned his gaze to the wall. There was little Chris had encountered in his short life that scared him, little except the unique terror that gripped him at the thought of falling from such a height.

The wall had no ropes or harness, just the ugly grey holds jutting from the smooth stone. One mistake, and he would tumble back to the hard ground. If he was lucky, the fall might only wind him, but from the full forty feet…

He shuddered again as the trembling spread to his whole body. It wasn't even the thought of injury that had him frozen – he'd been hurt countless times sparring at his Taekwondo Dojang – it was the thought of those few moments falling, of tumbling through the air, helpless to save himself.

"Chris!" He swung around as a voice shouted from the across the field. Sam had stopped in the middle of the running track and stood watching him. Their eyes met, and Chris saw the urgency there as he called again. "Climb!"

Before Chris could reply, Sam set off once more, leaving him alone with the doctor and the tower.

Except Chris no longer felt quite so alone. Another glance around the field, and he saw Ashley give a little wave, even caught what might have been the slightest of nods from Liz. He swallowed, their encouragement swelling in his chest. For a second, the terror seemed to recede, and he stepped up to the wall and took a firm grip of the first hold.

Hand over hand, Chris hauled himself up as the doctor watched on from below. The first ten feet were relatively easy, but as he went higher, Chris's terror came creeping back. Nearing halfway, he made the mistake of glancing down. Twenty feet of open air opened up beneath him, and he gripped his holds tighter, pulling himself tight against the wall.

He stayed frozen there for a long while, eyes squeezed shut, listening to the sounds of movement coming from around the field. He imagined Sam and Ashley and Liz watching him, heard their silent encouragement, but so far off the ground, the thought no longer held the same power. With each passing moment his terror grew, fed by the gulf beneath him, his imagination already playing out the fall that would see him tumble helplessly to the earth.

"Are you done, candidate?" the doctor called from below.

Candidate.

The word rung in Chris's mind, reminding him of what these people thought of him. He and the other prisoners were just numbers to these doctors, failed examples of humanity that served no purpose but to die in whatever horrible experiments they had in mind. Anger flared in Chris's chest, burning at the terror, and gritting his teeth, Chris started upwards once more.

Towards the top, the handholds became smaller and more sparse, forcing Chris to study his path carefully. His arms were burning from the exertion, but his rage gave him strength, and he continued up, clinging to the tiny holds like his life depended on it.

By the last ten feet, the holds were barely large enough for two fingers to hold. His whole body trembling and his breath coming in raged gasps, Chris forced himself onwards. He refused to look down, knowing it would only serve to feed the terror still nibbling at his insides, though eventually would need to if he was to climb back down.

Straining his leg to reach a better foothold, a sudden cramp tore through his calf. Crying out, Chris almost lost his holds from the shock of the pain. His leg spasmed and he stretched it out, struggling to keep his grip with just three points of contact for support. Slowly the pain dwindled, and taking a breath, Chris found a new foothold and continued.

When he finally reached the top, Chris experienced a moment of panic as his hand reached up and found only empty air. It took him several seconds of fumbling blinding around above his head before he caught the lip of the wall. A wave of relief swept over him, and using both hands, he pulled himself up and levered himself onto the top of the tower.

His heart pounding in his ears, Chris sucked in a breath and looked around. The tower rose above the walls of the facility, and from his vantage point he could see beyond the training field to the lands beyond their prison.

A heavy fog had swept in with the afternoon,

obscuring much of his view, but Chris could still see enough to feel the harsh fingers of despair clawing at his throat. Above the white clinging to the barren earth, towering mountains rose around the facility, their jagged peaks capped with snow.

Wherever they had been brought, it was a long way from civilization. Even if they managed to escape their prison, where would they go? In such a remote landscape, it would not take long for the elements to claim them. Even if they somehow survived the cold, they would soon starve in the barren land.

"Excellent work," the doctor's voice carried up to Chris, slicing through his despair.

He felt a strong urge to hurl himself from the tower and crash down on the man. From the such a height, the impact would probably kill them both. It might have been worth it, but just the thought had Chris gripping the stone beneath him tighter.

"Down you come then," his overseer continued, returning his attention to the e-tablet the doctors seemed to carry everywhere with them.

Chris swallowed. The way down was going to be even worse. He would have to be continuously looking down in search of the next hold. There would be no ignoring the open air beneath him. Feeling the fear returning, he looked around the field. The eyes of his friends were turned in his direction, and he recalled Ashley's words from back in their cell.

We are in this together now. We're family, you and I. All of us.

Nodding to each of them, Chris tightened his grip on the wall and levered himself over the edge. The climb down seemed to take an age, and even in last ten feet Chris dared not release the wall for fear of his body crumpling on impact with the ground.

When he finally stepped down onto the field, his legs were shaking so badly they almost gave way beneath him. He stumbled a step before recovering, then straightened and faced the doctor.

"So, doc, what's next?"

Liz lay in the darkness, eyes open, staring into empty space. Somewhere above was the concrete ceiling, but in the pitch-black she imagined it was the sky that stretched overhead, infinite in its expanse. Only there were no stars, no moon or drifting satellites, and in her heart, she could not convince herself of the illusion.

In her heart, she remained trapped, locked away within the soulless walls of the facility.

She could still feel the boy watching her, begging for help, for an end to the torture. A shudder ran through her as she remembered the way Halt had looked at her, the piercing grey of his eyes as he weighed her worth. It had been so close, a different toss of the coin, and he might have chosen her…

Biting back a sob, Liz closed her eyes, though it made no difference in the dark. She had wanted to go to him; only Ashley had stopped her. Instead, she had stood in silence, hand in hand with the girl from the city, as William slid towards death.

Liz shivered, a scream building in her throat. She bit it back, and drew the thin blanket closer around her. Goosebumps pricked her skin as she rolled onto her side. Her body ached and a constant thudding came from her temples. The doctors had subjected them to eight hours of relentless exercise, until the sun had finally dipped below the towering walls. By then, her body had been little more than a series of bruises. A measly meal of broiled stew in their cell had followed, though in truth it was better than most of what she'd scavenged in Sacramento. Then the lights had clanked off, plunging them into the darkness.

"You okay, Liz?" Ashley whispered from below.

Liz suppressed a shudder.

Am I okay? She turned the question over in her mind, wondering whether she would ever be okay again. At the thought, a yearning rose within her, a need for companionship, for comfort.

"I'm alive," she replied, then: "What about you?"

Out on the field, Ashley had barely moved while William lay writhing in the dirt. Her face had remained impassive; the only sign anything was amiss her iron-like grip around Liz's hand. Afterwards, Ashley had moved through the drills and tasks set by the doctors with an eerie calm, as though her mind were far away, detached from the horror of her situation.

There was a long pause before Ashley answered. "I'm alive too." Her breath quickened. "That's saying a lot."

"How long…how long have you and Sam been here?"

Another pause. "Weeks, a month. I've lost count of the days."

"And…and you've seen things like that, like today with William?"

Below, Ashley gave a sharp snort. "That, and more." She shifted in the bed, causing the bunk to rock.

Liz shivered, thinking of the icy glances that had passed between Ashley and Sam, as well as the others. "What about the two in the other group, Richard and Jasmine?"

"What about them?" Ashley's response was abrupt, her voice sharp.

"You know them," Liz whispered, aware she was treading on dangerous ground. "Who are they?"

"You'll find out soon enough, Liz. Best you not worry about it."

Liz swallowed. Ashley's reply brooked no argument, and an uneasy silence fell between them. For a while, Liz lay still, staring into space, wondering at Ashley's words. Below, Sam gave a snort and rolled in his bed. Liz stifled a groan as a rumble came from the boy's chest and he started to snore.

"The boys don't seem to be having any trouble sleeping," she muttered, hoping Ashley was still awake.

"You know what boys are like," came Ashley's reply. Liz could almost hear the girl smiling. "Emotional capacity of a brick and all…" Her voice faded for a moment. "Sam…he closes it off I think, buries it deep. It comes out in other ways though, like how he reacted to Chris when you arrived."

"And you?" Liz couldn't help but dig deeper. Through the heat and torture, the agonizing exercises and the hard-faced stares of the doctors, Ashley had not missed a beat. She had smiled through each new challenge, as though privy to some secret joke, moving with that same fluid grace Liz had noted when she'd first seen her.

When Ashley did not answer, Liz pressed on. "You looked so calm, even when…" She trailed off as William's agonized face reappeared in her mind.

"I was?" Ashley sounded surprised. Sheets rustled in the darkness. "I wasn't. Inside I was screaming, but I've learned when to keep things to myself, when not to draw attention. Even before this place, it was a skill I'd mastered."

Liz sat up at that. "What do you mean?"

Quiet laughter came from below. "I've had a lot

of practice, Liz. My parents worked for the government."

An icy hand slid its way down Liz's throat and wrapped its fingers around her heart. Her breath stuttered, the cold steel pressing against her throat. She grasped at the covers, tearing at the cheap fabric.

Below, Ashley was still talking. "They worked in media relations, of all things. No one important, nothing to do with the President and his people. Just a couple of analysts in a tiny department of our fine administration." Her last sentence rang with sarcasm. "But even two lowly analysts quickly discovered there's no such thing as free speech these days. *Especially* for those close to power. They had to learn to wear masks, to hide their true beliefs about the goings-on of the government. By the time my older sister and I came along, they had become masters at it. So I guess you could say, I learned from the best."

"Why would they stay?" Liz tried to keep the emotion from her voice, but the question came out harsh, accusing.

"Why?" Ashley paused, as though considering the question. "For my sister and me, I guess. To give us a better life. They may not have agreed with everything the government did, but they knew leaving was not really an option. Their careers would have been destroyed. They didn't want to raise their daughters on the streets."

"Yes, it's not much of a life," Liz all but growled.

Ashley fell silent, and for a long while it seemed she would not reply. Guilt welled in Liz's chest, but she pushed it down.

"Didn't really matter in the end, did it? They sacrificed their beliefs, their integrity, so we could live, but it didn't make any difference. They were found out for doing something wrong, I guess. Must have been, because here I am."

Liz's anger dwindled with Ashley's words. It was not the girl's fault she'd been born into wealth, while Liz had been condemned to the poverty-stricken countryside. Even so, she could not quite set aside the emotion, could not quite let it go.

"Sorry," she offered at last, her tone still harsh. "It's just, for as long as I can remember, the government has been the enemy. Even as a child, they were the people who came and took our food, the landowners who held our lives in the palm of their hands. Then, when I was older, after my parents… after they passed…" She shook her head, angry images flashing through her mind.

"I understand," Ashley's whisper came from below. "But none of that matters now, does it? Whoever our parents were, whatever we've been through, we've arrived in the same place. We're both trapped in the same nightmare. You'll learn that, soon enough."

"It gets worse?" Liz spoke the words without emotion. Her energy was spent, and she could hardly bring herself to care about whatever fresh trials the morning might bring.

"Only if you're human," Ashley replied.

The words rang with finality and Liz sensed the conversation had come to an end. Shivering, she hugged the covers tight around her. Suddenly she longed to be wrapped in another's arms, to be touched by another human. An image of her mother drifted into her thoughts, a warm smile on her lips, eyes dancing with humor.

Biting back a cry, Liz buried her head in the pillow, anxious to hide her sorrow. As she cried, another thought rose, a question that demanded an answer. One she should have asked. Silently, she cursed her selfish grief.

"Ashley," she breathed. "What happened to your sister?"

Silence clung to the darkness, and long minutes passed, until Liz was sure the girl had already fallen asleep.

"She's dead." The answer came just as Liz was preparing to give up.

Sobs came from below, carrying with them the pain of loss.

"I'm sorry," Liz whispered, the words hollow, even to her.

Ashley did not reply, and Liz lay back on her bed, listening as Ashley's crying faded away.

It was a long time before sleep found Liz.

❧ 16 ❧

Liz stumbled as she entered the room, the sudden, brilliant light blinding her. Stars danced across her vision as behind her, the door slammed closed. She jumped at the sound, and almost tripped, before managing to right herself. Straightening, she blinked again and finally took in her surroundings.

Overhead, fluorescent bulbs lined the ceiling, filling the room with their distant whine. Otherwise, the room was unlike anything she'd seen so far. Three walls were covered by white padding, while the third shone with silver glass, its surface reflecting her tangled hair. She shivered, seeing the exhaustion in her eyes, the bruises marking her cheeks.

For three days, the doctors had taken them to the outdoor field and driven them through an endless series of tests and exercises. Unused to the strain, Liz had quickly learned that failure meant pain. She had been forced to dig deep within herself, to stores of strength she hadn't known she possessed, in order to survive. But now things had changed again.

She took another step into the room, the soft floor yielding beneath her feet. Turning from what she guessed was a one-way mirror, she faced the boy standing in the center of the room. His long blond hair hung in dirty clumps around his face, where purple bruises matched Liz's own. He bit his lip, his eyes flickering around the room, uncertainty writ in his every gesture. Behind him was another door, its surface padded like the one through which she had entered.

Joshua, she thought, recalling his name from their first day on the training field.

He looked at her as she thought his name. "What's going on?" he croaked.

Liz shrugged and shook her head. "I don't know, Joshua."

They had not spoken since that first day. Ashley and Sam had been insistent, refusing to even acknowledge the other group of inmates. Somehow, Liz did not think their rule applied now.

Before either of them could speak further, a loud squeal interrupted them. Liz winced, the hairs on her neck standing up as a crackling voice followed.

"Welcome," the voice began, coming from somewhere in the ceiling. "Congratulations on surviving this far. As you know, only the strongest are needed for the final stages of our experiment."

Liz crossed her arms and turned to face the mirror. Raising an eyebrow, she rolled her eyes so those behind could see. She was sick of listening to these people, sick of them acting like they owned her. Collar or no, she refused to be treated like an animal any longer, to bend to their will.

The voice ignored her display of insolence and continued: "Unfortunately, time constraints require us to press on. This phase of the project must be completed by week's end. That means omitting the standard rest period for new subjects such as yourselves."

"Hardly seems fair," Liz muttered under her breath, flashing a quick grin at Joshua.

Joshua shrugged and cast another uncertain look at the glass. They stood in silence, waiting for the voice to continue. "Regretfully, we must cull our population of candidates for our next phase. Only the strongest would survive the final process regardless, and we do not have the resources to waste on failed specimens. Thus, only the best will survive today."

Liz shuddered at the casual way the voice described ending their lives. She recalled the faces lining the corridor outside their cell. Some of them might have been as young as thirteen. Their whole lives were ahead of them. And these people wished to snuff them out, to slaughter them like they were no more than field mice beneath their boots.

Joshua seemed a little younger than her, maybe seventeen years old. He was a little taller too, and bulkier, with the broad shoulders of a swimmer. His amber eyes were watching her now, his fear shining out like a beacon.

"Only one of you will leave that room alive. You must decide for yourselves whether you possess the will to live. To the victor, goes life."

Liz glanced from the mirror to Joshua and back. She sought out some sign of the watchers beyond, but the glass showed only the horror on her face. And the boy's wide eyes, the hardening of his brow, his fists clenching as he faced her.

Whatever her own thoughts, Joshua had clearly already made up his mind.

Only if you're human. Ashley's words from their midnight conversation returned to her.

They weighed on Liz's soul as she watched Joshua, saw his muscles tensing. In that moment, she knew in her heart that she too would do whatever was necessary to survive.

The fear had already fallen from Joshua's face. His eyes weighed her up. A smile spread across his lips as he realized his chances of victory were high. There was no question who the doctors expected to survive.

He stepped towards her, and Liz quickly

retreated. She studied him as they circled one another, searching for a weakness. It was easy to see she could not match his strength, but she was light on her feet and hoped he might prove overconfident. After two years on the streets, wandering between towns and cities, Liz was no stranger to a fight.

Yet with the padded walls ringing her in, there would be no room to run if she made a mistake. If he caught her in his long arms, it would all be over. Though his capacity for murder was yet to be tested, she had no desire be at his mercy.

She certainly would not be giving him any second chances.

Joshua gave a shout and leapt towards her, eating up the space between them in a single stride. Liz twisted as he came for her, jumping backwards to avoid his flailing arms, and smiled as he staggered past. Despite his greater size, the boy was no fighter.

Maybe she had a chance after all.

Joshua came to a stop near the wall and spun to face her. A wicked scowl crossed his face. Liz swallowed hard and braced herself.

Raising her fists, she nodded. "Let's get this over with then."

A low growl came from Joshua as he started forward again, his footsteps controlled now, each movement carefully measured. Liz spread her feet wide and slid one foot backwards, readying herself.

She had no intention of letting him get close enough to grab her, but he needed to be a *little* closer yet.

As Joshua took another step, she screamed and hurled herself forward. His eyes widened, but close as they were, he had no time to react. Liz slammed her fist into the center of his chest, aiming for the solar plexus.

Air exploded between the boy's teeth and he staggered backwards, a half-choked groan rattling from his throat. The color fled his face as he clutched his chest, mouth wide and gasping.

Watching his distress, Liz hesitated, guilt welling within her. Joshua hadn't been expecting her to fight back, certainly not with such sudden violence. But as he bent in two, wheezing in the cold air, she knew she could not spare him. If he recovered, he would not fall for the same trick twice.

Doubled over, Joshua's head provided the perfect target. Liz clasped her hands together and brought them down on the back of his head.

Joshua's legs buckled and he slammed into the ground without a sound. His arms splayed out on either side of him and a muffled groan came from his mouth. Relief swept through Liz at the sound—at least she hadn't killed him. Maybe they would allow him to live. After all, they couldn't have expected her to win this matchup.

Turning to the one-way mirror, she raised an

eyebrow in question. As she did, Joshua's hand shot out and grabbed her by the leg.

Liz screamed as fingers like steel closed around her ankle and yanked, sending her crashing to the ground. The shock of the fall drove the breath from her lungs, and she gasped, struggling to breathe. Pain shot through her ankle as the fingers squeezed. Cursing, she kicked out with her foot, but Joshua surged forward and caught it in his other hand.

Panic clutched Liz's stomach as she fought to break his grip. Sucking in a lungful of air, she tried to roll away, but his hands held her like iron shackles. However hard she strained, they refused to give. Joshua's teeth flashed as his lips drew back in a grin.

In a sudden rush, he dragged her across the floor, pulling himself up as he did so. He released her, but before she could squirm free, Joshua's weight crashed down on her chest, pinning her down.

Hands fumbled at her throat, fingernails tearing at her skin.

Liz lashed out with a fist, catching Joshua in the side of the head. He reeled sideways, but his weight did not shift and she failed to break free.

Recovering his balance, Joshua snarled and raised a fist. Liz raised her arm in time to deflect the blow, but a scream tore from her lips as it glanced from her shoulder. She swung at him again, but there was no strength in the blow this time and it bounced weakly off his chin.

Liz was not so lucky.

Stars exploded across her vision as Joshua's fist connected with her forehead. Her head thudded back into the soft ground. Distantly, she thought how considerate it was for the doctors to have provided a padded floor while their prisoners beat each other to death. Then another blow slammed into her jaw, and the fight went from her in a sudden rush. Darkness spun at the edges of Liz's vision.

Cold fear spread through her stomach as a tentative hand wrapped around her neck. She sucked in a breath as the pressure closed around her throat. Panicked, she stared up at Joshua, silently pleading for mercy.

Joshua stared back, his eyes hard, lips drawn back in a snarl, teeth clenched in rage. Whoever he'd been before entering this room, that Joshua was long gone. He'd been burned away, the innocence of the boy replaced by anger, by bitter hatred, by the desperation to live.

Fire grew in Liz's chest, willing her to action. She kicked feebly, trying to maneuver herself into a position to attack. But his weight was far beyond her strength to lift. Before she could struggle further, he lifted her head and slammed it back into the ground. Despite the spongy surface, Liz's vision spun.

She opened her mouth, gasping in desperation, but the pressure did not relent and she managed only a whisper of a breath. Darkness filled the edges of her vision as every muscle in her body began to scream. Bit by bit her strength slipped away, replaced by the endless burning of suffocation.

On top of her, Joshua leaned closer, eyes wide with vicious intent.

In that moment, Liz saw her opening.

He was so close, just inches away. She could not miss. With the last of her strength, she clenched her fist and drove it up into Joshua's throat. The steel rim of the collar bit into her knuckles, but behind it, she felt something give, something fracture with the force of her blow.

The pressure around her throat vanished as Joshua toppled backwards. A low gurgling echoed off the walls as he gasped, his hands going to his own neck, his legs thrashing against the soft floor.

Liz sucked in glorious breath, her throat aching from the icy air. She struggled to her hands and knees, still coughing and wheezing. Her head swirled and the room spun, but she dug her nails into the spongy floor and willed herself to remain conscious.

Get up, Liz!

Slowly, Liz pulled herself to her feet and stood swaying in the center of the room. The white lights burned her eyes, blinding her, but she clenched her fists, and by sheer will stayed upright.

She looked down at Joshua, bracing herself to continue the fight. Her stomach lurched when she saw him.

Joshua no longer moved, no longer thrashed, no longer breathed. His mouth hung open, and his eyes were wide and staring, but the boy within was gone. His face was a mottled white and purple, the veins of his neck bulging, and a black bruise was already spreading from beneath his collar.

Joshua lay dead at her feet.

Tears ran from Liz's eyes as she sank to the ground.

The darkness came rushing up to meet her.

❧ 17 ❧

Chris watched as William staggered upright, his heart sinking at the thought of fighting another round with the sickly boy. To his relief, William's strength failed him, and he toppled forward, landing with an undignified *thud* on the padded floor.

Closing his eyes, Chris let out a long sigh.

It's over.

The thought was scant comfort. In the end, it hadn't been much of a fight. William was tall and had long arms, but there was not a scrap of muscle on him. And he had never quite recovered from that first day on the field. Young and inexperienced, he had attacked Chris first, but his heart had never been in it, and Chris had easily deflected his clumsy blows.

Crossing his arms, Chris had looked at the glass, and shaken his head in defiance.

A harsh beep had come from his collar, followed by a bolt of electricity that sent Chris to his knees. Gasping, he reached for his throat, but the shock had already ceased.

The voice had come again as Chris regained his feet.

"That was your only warning. Engage with your opponent, or forfeit your life."

Out of options, Chris had obeyed. Despite their captor's command, Chris had held back, pulling his blows where he could. But as the fight progressed, William had grown desperate, fighting harder, and Chris had been forced to act.

A kick to William's head had sent him reeling, and he'd never recovered.

Now Chris waited, guilt eating at his stomach, curdling the measly remnants of his breakfast. He stared into the mirrored glass, struggling to pierce the reflection, to find the faces of their tormentors. Whoever they were, Chris hated them with a violence he had not thought himself capable of.

The door behind William opened with the whisper of oiled hinges. Two guards entered, followed by a woman in a white lab coat. His heart lurched—but then he realized the woman was not Fallow. One of the guards checked on William, while the other approached Chris, gesturing him back against the wall.

Once the doctor was satisfied both prisoners were

secure, she strode across the room to the fallen boy. A wireless headset was wrapped around her left ear, half hidden by the curls of her auburn hair. She spoke as she moved, transmitting observations to whoever was on the other end. In one hand, she carried a sleek steel instrument.

Chris shivered as he recognized the jet injector, identical to the one Fallow had used on him the night he'd been taken.

The doctor crouched beside William, still talking into her headset. The boy was on his hands and knees, struggling to find his balance. The woman laid a hand on his shoulder.

"Subject is still conscious. He appears to be suffering from a concussion. Assessment?"

A low groan came from William as he turned towards the woman. "Wha…what happened?"

Chris closed his eyes, guilt welling within him. He had seen these same symptoms in his Taekwondo Dojang, when younger fighters got carried away sparring without wearing their head guards. Still, he didn't think he'd hit William that hard, just enough to take the fight out of him.

The doctor was nodding to the voice in her ear. "Affirmative. There would be no purpose in resuming the fight. Administering the injection."

Before Chris could react, the woman leaned down and pressed the jet injector to William's neck. The hiss of gas followed as the vial attached to the gun emptied. Quickly, she withdrew the gun, stood, and retreated across the room.

Still on the ground, William raised a hand to his neck in bewilderment.

The woman watched on, her face impassive, arms crossed and fingers tapping against her elbow.

Whatever had been in the injection did not take long to work. Chris stood frozen in place as William started to cough. Then, without warning, his eyes rolled back in his skull. A violent shudder went through him as he took a desperate gasp, as though he were sucking air through a straw. He bent over, groaning, his mouth moving as though he were trying to speak. Wild eyes flickered around the room, pleading for help.

The spell broke as Chris's gaze met William's. He started forward, but the outstretched arm of a guard barred his way. Before Chris could slip past, the man grasped him by the shirt and tossed him back against the wall. The pads broke the impact, but Chris staggered as he landed and barely kept his feet.

He looked up in time to see William pitch face-first into the ground, a low moan marking his final exhalation of breath. His feet kicked for a second longer, then stilled. Silence fell across the room as the guard stepped back from Chris and faced the doctor.

The woman crouched again beside William. She touched a finger to his neck, then gave a curt nod.

"Subject has expired. Subject Christopher

Sanders is cleared for advancement." The words were spoken without emotion, as though she were discussing the weather.

"*Why?*" Chris screamed.

The woman looked up quickly, her eyes widening. The guards edged forwards, placing themselves between Chris and the doctor.

"Why?" Chris said again, taking another step.

The woman's surprise faded, though her eyes flickered to the guards before she addressed him. "He was weak. He would not have survived Phase Two. This was the humane option."

"*Humane?*" Chris clenched his fists. "He was helpless!"

"Because of his concussion, he passed without knowing what was happening," The doctor spoke with a calm efficiency, as though explaining something to a child.

A wild anger took Chris then, an impossible rage that swept away all caution. He leapt without thinking, fingers reaching for the woman's throat. The guards raced to intercept him, but Chris never made it that far.

Agony tore through his neck, spreading instantly to his every muscle, taking his feet out from under him. He screamed as he struck the ground, and felt the pain of a thousand needles stabbing him. His head thumped against something solid as a convulsion rippled through him. The reek of burning flesh reached his nostrils and his back arched.

When the agony finally ceased, he found himself staring up at the ceiling. The bright light sliced through his skull, and he quickly closed his eyes again.

Movement came from nearby, followed by a voice. "Try that again, and we will find someone else to take your place."

Chris opened his eyes to find the woman standing over him. She held a finger over her watch, a ready smile twisting her lips.

He nodded, swallowing hard as the collar pressed against his throat.

"This is for the greater good, Christopher," the doctor continued. "Without us, you would already be dead. At least here, we have given you a fighting chance. Trust me when I say the government interrogators are not nearly as humane."

She stood then, waving a hand at the guards. "Get him up."

Rough hands grasped Chris beneath his shoulders and hauled him to his feet. He stumbled as they held him, struggling to control his legs. They jerked and twitched, refusing to obey, but eventually he got them firmly on the ground. Even so, the guards did not release him, perhaps knowing from experience how unstable he was.

"Bring him," the woman said as she turned and opened the door.

Chris's gaze lingered on the dead boy as the guards dragged him from the room. William still lay where he had fallen, still and silent, eyes wide and staring from the lifeless husk of his body.

Then they were outside, marching back down long white corridors. Distantly, Chris thought they were heading for the cells, but he paid no attention to his surroundings. His mind was elsewhere, locked away in the room with William, the dead eyes still staring at him.

It's your fault. The thought ate at him.

William had never stood a chance. The minute they'd entered the room, the boy's life had been forfeit. These people had known it, had wanted it to happen.

Doors slammed as they moved deeper into the facility. He knew where they were heading now, that he would soon find himself back in the tiny cell. The others would be waiting for him. And they would know, would see the truth in his eyes.

That he was a killer.

❦ 18 ❦

The steel door to the prison block appeared ahead, the guards outside already opening it. In a blink, Chris and his captors were through, and they were marching him down the rows of cells. Only a few faces remained now to watch Chris's return.

On first glimpse, Chris thought his cell was empty. He felt a second's relief, that he might not yet have to face the accusations of his cellmates, but as the guard drew the door open, he glimpsed movement from Liz's bed. Her haggard face poked into view, and she watched in grim silence as the guards propelled Chris inside.

Steel screeched behind him, followed by the *clang* of the locking mechanism. Footsteps retreated down the corridor, fading until another *clang* announced the guards' departure from the prison block.

Standing there, Chris's legs began to shake. Gasping, he gripped the metal bar of his bunk, struggling to stay upright. He closed his eyes, waiting for Liz to speak, to hurl her accusations.

You killed him.

The words screamed in his mind, but Liz remained silent. Only the distant whisper of other prisoners could be heard. He took a deep breath, tasting the bleach in the air, the blood from a cut on his lip.

"Are you okay?" He jumped as Liz finally spoke.

He looked up then, finding Liz's big eyes watching him, and saw his own pain reflected in their sapphire depths. She sat on her bunk, knuckles white as she gripped the metal sidebar. Her eyes shone, and a single tear streaked her cheek.

"No." Chris's shoulders slumped. "You?"

She shook her head, looked away, but he had seen the guilt in her eyes. The truth hung over the room like a blanket, smothering them.

They were alive. And that could only mean one thing.

Chris took a better grip of his bunk and hauled himself up. Crawling across the sagging mattress, he collapsed into his pillow. Then he turned and saw Liz still watching him. Her lips trembled. There was no sign of the proud, defiant girl he'd first seen in the cages. The last few days, last few hours, had broken her.

Broken us both, a voice reminded him.

Chris pushed himself up and twisted to face Liz. "Did you…?" His voice trailed off. He couldn't finish the question.

Her crystal eyes found his. "Yes," she whispered.

A chill went through Chris at her words. He stared at her, noticing now the purple bruise on her cheek, the dried blood on her lip. His eyes travelled lower and found the swollen black skin beneath her collar. He shuddered. Her struggle had been far more real than his. He remembered the boy Joshua, guessed he was the one…

"What happened?" he asked.

Liz closed her eyes. "I didn't mean…" She sucked in a breath, and her eyes flashed open. "I didn't *want* to," she growled.

Chris nodded, leaning back against the concrete wall. "You did what you had to."

"He would have killed me," she continued as though he had not spoken. "I had to do it. He left me no choice…"

Chris felt a sudden urge to wrap his arms around the young woman, to hold her until the pain left her. This was a side of Liz he had not seen, a vulnerability beneath the armor she'd worn from the first moment he'd laid eyes on her. Gone was the hardness, the distant air of superiority. The foulness of this place had consumed everything else, had reduced them both to shadows of their former selves.

He could almost feel his humanity fading away, slipping through his fingers like grains of rice. With each fresh atrocity he witnessed, with every awful thing they forced him to do, he lost another part of himself, took one step closer to becoming the animal they thought him to be. One way or another, soon he would cease to exist. Nothing would remain of the boy his mother had raised.

"It doesn't matter," Chris said. Liz looked up at his words, and he continued, his voice breaking. "Whether you killed him or not, only one of you was ever walking out of that room. After my…after William fell, he couldn't stand, couldn't defend himself. A doctor came. She executed him."

A sharp hiss of breath came from Liz, but it was a long time before she replied. "Who are these people?"

Monsters, Chris thought, but did not speak the word.

Across from him, Liz started to cough. A long, drawn-out series of wheezes and gasps rattled from her chest, going on and on, until her face was flushed red and her brow creased with pain. Finally, she leaned back against the wall, panting for breath.

"Are you okay?" Chris whispered.

Liz opened her eyes and stared at him. "Of course, city boy. I can take a beating."

Chris winced. His own anger rose but he bit back a curt reply. There was no point taking offense. He could see her pain, knew where the anger came from. He had not missed the coldness with which she addressed himself and their cellmates at times, her hesitation to join their conversations.

Another rattle came from her chest as she laid her head back against the wall.

"We're not all bad, you know," he said at last. "Not all rich, either. There are a lot of people who disagree with the government now, even in the cities. There have been protests…"

"Protests?" Liz coughed, her voice wry. "Well, nice to hear you're getting out."

Chris sighed. "I understand—"

"You don't," Liz said, cutting him off. "You think you do, but you don't. You can't. Because while you lived your cozy life in the city, I was forced onto the streets. Not because I wanted to, not because I had a choice, but because everyone I knew was dead. Slaughtered."

Shivering, Chris opened his mouth to reply, then thought better of it.

Liz eyed him for a moment before continuing: "I had nowhere to go, no one left to turn to. I thought the police would help, that they would protect me. But when they came, they looked at me like I was nothing, like I was an inconvenience to them. They would have arrested me, thrown me in some place like this if I hadn't run."

Chris looked away from the pain in Liz's eyes. He

stared at his hands, the bruises on his knuckles. His stomach clenched with guilt.

"I'm sorry," he whispered at last. "You shouldn't have been treated that way. It's not right." He paused. "Was it a *Chead*?"

Liz flinched at the word. When she did not reply, Chris went on. "Mom always said something needed to be done, that her father would have been ashamed with what's happened since the war. We should never have let things get so bad." He took a breath. "But that doesn't change what I said. We're not all evil, Liz. Some of us want to fix things, want the government to be held accountable."

"So I should just give all of you the benefit of the doubt? For decades you ignored the *Chead*, let them terrorize the countryside. You only cared when they came for you." Liz snapped.

"No," Chris replied softly. "You should judge us by our own actions, not those of others." He breathed out. "A long time ago, I might have hated you too, Liz. Feared you for being different, for speaking with a rural accent."

"But not now?"

He shook his head. "No..." He trailed off, remembering a time long ago. "When I was younger, I was running late getting home from school. It was getting dark, and we don't live in a good neighborhood. When I was nearly home, a man stepped out of an alleyway. He had a knife."

"Let me guess, he was from the country too?"

Chris laughed softly. "No, he spoke like a normal person." He couldn't help but tease her for the assumption. "But I think he was an addict of some sort—his eyes were wild and his hands were shaking. Before I had a chance to reach for my bag, he swung the knife at me, caught me in the shoulder. I still have the scar…"

Liz nodded. "I saw."

Chris glanced across at her, his cheeks warming. He remembered his embarrassment when they'd been forced to remove their clothes. Apparently, Liz had allowed her eyes to roam more than he had.

"What does this have to do with anything, Chris?"

Chris shrugged. "I think he would have killed me if someone else hadn't come along." He paused, looking across at Liz. "I don't know where he came from, but suddenly there was a man standing between us. *He* spoke with a rural accent, told the mugger to leave. When the man didn't listen, my rescuer took his knife away and sent him running."

"And this suddenly changed your mind about us?"

Chris shrugged. "Not overnight, no. But the man walked me home, right to my front door. He even helped mom with my wound. He didn't have to help me, could have left me to die, dismissed me as some spoiled brat who deserved it. But he chose to help me instead. Since then, I've tried to do the same. To give people a chance, whoever they are."

Liz let out a long sigh. "And you want the same from me now?" she asked. "Because some man from the country saved you from a mugger?"

Chris chuckled. "It would be nice to start with a clean slate."

"After today, I'm not sure that's possible for us, Chris. Joshua's blood is on my hands…"

"No," Chris replied firmly. "It's on theirs."

Liz nodded, but they both knew the words meant little. They might not have had a choice, but that did little to lessen the burden.

"We're all in this together now, aren't we?" Liz repeated Ashley's words from all those days ago, on the day they had arrived.

Chris's gut clenched as he realized that she and Sam still had not returned.

On the other bed, Liz continued, her voice hesitant. "Okay, Chris," she whispered. "I'll give you a chance."

"Thank you," he said after a while.

Silence settled around them then. Chris stared up at the ceiling, struggling to resolve the emotions battling within him. William's face drifted through his thoughts, his eyes wide and staring, but the guilt felt a little less now. Liz had faced the same question, given the same answer.

Somehow, that made things just a little easier to bear.

Long hours ticked past and the others did not return. Chris and Liz waited in the hushed stillness of the cell, listening to the thump of the guard's boots outside, the whisper of voices from the other cells. Liz's breath grew more ragged.

Finally, the bang of the outer door announced the arrival of newcomers. The soft tread of footsteps followed, moving down the corridor. Metal screeched as cell doors opened, and the footsteps continued on towards them.

Chris sat up as shadows fell across the bars of their cell. Relief swelled in his chest when he saw Ashley and Sam standing outside. Hinges squeaked as the door opened and they stumbled inside. Sad smiles touched their faces as they saw Chris and Liz.

"So," Sam breathed. "You're alive."

❧ 19 ❧

Angela shoved the door to Halt's office open without pausing to knock and strode inside. She glimpsed surprise on the harsh lines of her supervisor's face as he looked up, though it vanished by the time the door slammed shut behind her. Anger took its place as Halt half-rose from his chair, fists clenched hard on his desk.

"What—?"

"You have no right!" Angela yelled, cutting him off.

Halt straightened. "I have every right," he said, his voice low, dangerous.

Hands trembling, Angela approached his desk. "It's not ready, Halt," she hissed. "You can't start those trials tomorrow. I need more time."

Rising, Halt walked around his desk, until he stood towering over her. Angela stared back, defiant, anger feeding her strength. She had just learned Halt planned to initiate the next phase of the project tomorrow. The same project she had dedicated the last five years of her life to.

"The Director wants results, Doctor Fallow," Halt said between clenched teeth, "and you've been stalling."

Angela refused to back down. "I've been doing my job," she snapped, "and I'm telling you, *the virus is not ready!*"

Halt smiled. "I've looked over your work, Fallow." Angela shivered at his tone. "And I say it's ready. After all, fortune favors the bold."

The words of the old Latin proverb curled around Angela's mind as she stepped back. They reminded her of Halt during her early days. The government had sent him to her after she'd discovered the truth about the *Chead*, bringing her their new virus.

Angela drew in a breath to steady herself. "There are still problems with the uptake," she said. "You could kill them all with your recklessness."

"The alterations will work—"

"Of course they will," Angela interrupted. "Animal trials have shown us as much. It's their immune response that concerns me. Their bodies will tear themselves apart fighting the virus."

Halt waved a hand as he moved back behind his desk. "Should that eventuate, we will administer immunosuppressants until the chromosomal changes have set." He sat back at his desk, one eyebrow raised. "Is that all?"

"Immunosuppressants?" Angela pressed her palms against the desk and leaned in. "We'll have to move them to an isolation room, watch them around the clock. They wouldn't last a day in the cells."

"Whatever it takes, Fallow." Halt stared her down. "We can't wait any longer. The President himself wants answers. We'll be shut down if we don't provide them soon. The attacks are growing worse. The authorities are desperate."

"What?"

Halt leaned back in his chair. "We have underestimated the *Chead* for too long. The Director should have given us the funding we needed for this years ago. There was an attack in San Francisco yesterday. They've reached the capital, Fallow."

Doubt gnawed at Angela's chest at his words. "You really think this is the answer?"

"Of course." Halt regarded her with a detached curiosity. "Do not lose focus now, Doctor Fallow. Not when we're so close. This project will change everything. When we succeed, the Western Allied States will herald in a new era of human evolution. The *Chead* will be hunted down and eradicated, our enemies at home and abroad consigned to the pages of history."

Staring into her superior's eyes, Angela shuddered. Naked greed lurked in their grey depths. For the first time, she allowed herself to look around, to take in the grisly display lining the walls of Halt's office. The sight she had been doing her best to ignore.

Halt's office was lined with shelves, each holding dozens of jars filled with clear fluids. Suspended in the liquid within them were animals of every shape and size. Birds and lizards, cats and snakes and what looked like a platypus stared down at her, their eyes blank and dead. An opossum curled around its ringed tail on the shelf behind Halt's head, while beside it a baby chimpanzee hugged its chest. With its eyes closed, it might have been sleeping.

Angela looked away, struggling to hide her disgust from Halt.

"Soon they will all be obsolete," Halt commented, noticing her discomfort.

"Yes." She almost choked on the word.

But at what cost? she added silently.

Halt eyed her closely. "Was there anything else, Doctor Fallow?"

Angela shook her head. She knew when she was defeated. Turning, she all but ran from the room. She closed the door carefully behind her, her anger spent. Once outside, she placed a hand against the wall, shivering with sudden fear. Events were accelerating now, slipping beyond her control, and it was all she could do to keep up.

In her mind, she saw images of San Francisco, the steep roads teeming with life. She imagined the devastation a *Chead* would cause in such a place, the mindless slaughter. Bodies would pile up as police struggled to reach the scene through the traffic-clogged streets. How long might the *Chead* have run rampant?

Straightening, Angela turned from Halt's door and started down the corridor. Tomorrow, if they succeeded, the world would change. Humanity's evolution would take one giant leap forward, and one way or another, there would be no going back.

A sudden doubt rose within her, a fear for what was to come. What if they were wrong? What if they failed, and it was all for naught?

And what if they succeeded? What then?

Her skin tingled as she recalled Halt's words, heard again his triumphant declaration.

Our enemies, at home and abroad, will be consigned to the pages of history.

A cold breeze blew across Liz's neck, rustling the branches above her head. She picked up the pace, eyeing the lengthening shadows. She was close to home now, the path familiar beneath her feet, but it was a steep climb and she had no wish to attempt it in the dark.

The forest was eerily silent, the usual evening chorus of birds and insects mute. It put her on edge, and her eyes scanned the scraggly trees neighboring the path, seeking danger. Their dense branches shifted with the wind, but otherwise there was no sign of movement.

She moved on.

Behind her, the path wound down through the forest. The mountain on which their homestead perched stood alone amidst the Californian floodplains, looking out across their broad expanse. All around the rock were the lands of the Flores family—or at least the lands they managed. Once they'd been theirs, but no longer.

Liz smiled as she approached the final bend in the track. The house was only a thirty-minute walk up the mountain, but she was glad to see the end of it. It had been a long journey from San Francisco.

The trees opened out, revealing the homestead sitting at the trail's end. Liz listened for the first shouts of welcome. Her family employed a dozen laborers on the property, and most were like family to her.

Silence.

Liz shivered as she closed on the homestead. Her eyes flickered around the collection of buildings, searching for movement, for signs of life.

It was only then she saw the bodies.

They lay strewn across the ground, torn and broken, their faces grey and dead. Blood splattered the walls nearby, streaked across the peeling paint. She looked over the bodies, lingering on their faces. There was Nancy, the old woman who had helped raise her, who had cooked meals while her mother helped in the fields. And there, Henry, the man her father thought of as a brother.

Standing amidst the carnage, Liz turned to the building she called home. Without thinking, she started towards it. Her movements were jerky, her breath coming in desperate sobs. Reaching the old wooden door, she pushed it open.

It swung inwards without resistance, revealing the wreckage within. Swallowing a scream, Liz staggered inside, taking in the shattered plaster walls, the torn-up floorboards. Dust and rubble lay strewn across the floor, mingling with the blood pooling at the end of the corridor.

Barely daring to breathe, Liz stepped inside the house. With cautious footsteps, she slid down the corridor, her eyes fixed on the blood. She winced at each soft thump of her boots, the sound impossibly loud in the silent house.

The corner neared. In a sudden rush, Liz darted forward, desperate to see…

Liz screamed and threw up her arms, tearing herself from the nightmare. Her eyes snapped open, but absolute darkness blanketed her, and she screamed again, thrashing against the tangle of covers wrapped around her. She rolled, slamming into the safety bar. It groaned and gave way, and suddenly Liz was falling, a final scream tearing from her throat…

Thud.

Agony lanced through her arms as she struck the concrete. The last tendrils of the dream fell away, plunging her back into reality—and the pain that went with it. She groaned, her throat burning as it pressed against the cold steel of her collar.

"What?" a voice shouted, somewhere in the darkness.

"Who's there?" someone else yelled.

"Liz?" She recognized Chris's voice.

Above her, Chris's bunk rattled. Then hands were reaching for her, grasping her shoulder, pulling her up.

"Are you alright?" Chris's voice came again.

Half in shock, Liz couldn't manage more than a

nod. Distantly, she was surprised at the tenderness in his words, his sudden concern. A second later, she realized he could not see her nod. Opening her mouth, she managed a croak: "Yes."

As sanity slowly returned, embarrassment swept through Liz. She closed her eyes, silently berating herself for her panic. It had been so long since she'd had the dream—months, maybe even a year. Why had it returned now, after all this time?

"What happened?" Sam's voice was heavy with sleep.

"Sorry," Liz murmured, her heart still racing. "Just a bad dream."

"Some bad dream." Ashley's hand settled on her shoulder. "Go back to bed, Sam. You need your beauty sleep."

A string of inaudible mumbles came from Sam's bed, but was quickly followed by snoring.

Arms shaking, Liz pulled herself up, helped by Chris on one side, Ashley on the other.

"It's okay," she murmured and then suppressed a groan.

Her throat was aflame, throbbing with each beat of her heart. She tried to swallow, but it only made the pain worse. The steel collar dug into her swollen throat. Gasping, she fought for breath.

"What's wrong?" Chris asked in the darkness.

"My throat," Liz gasped.

"Water." Somehow, Chris understood. "Ashley, help me get her to the sink."

Sharp pain sliced Liz's shin where she'd landed as she tried to take her weight. With a silent moan, she collapsed against her friends. To her right, Ashley swore as the shift in weight sent her stumbling into the bed. Then she straightened, getting her body beneath Liz's shoulder, and helped her the few steps to the sink.

Liz slumped to the ground as Ashley released her. The sound of running water followed, while Chris helped her to sit comfortably.

"Here," Ashley whispered. "Open your mouth, Liz. The water will help."

Liz obeyed as Ashley fumbled at her face in the pitch-black. She almost lost an eye before Ashley finally found her lips. Cool water dribbled into her mouth, trickling from the palm of the girl's hands. Swallowing slowly, Liz sighed as the cold spread down her throat.

Ashley repeated the procedure three more times before Liz's breathing eased. At last she croaked for them to stop, and they settled together on Ashley's bed.

"How are you feeling now?" Ashley whispered.

In the other bed, Sam was still snoring. Listening in the darkness, Liz found herself jealous of the boy's ability to sleep through anything. She desperately needed the release of sleep, to escape the pain of her beaten body. But she knew it would not come now, not after the dream.

"I'm okay," she breathed. "You should go back to sleep."

A soft chuckle came from the girl. "My bed's a little crowded now. It's okay, I think the lights will turn on soon."

Her words were met by a distant clang, followed by a low buzzing in the ceiling. Liz blinked as white light flooded the room. She raised an eyebrow at Ashley, sitting beside her, yellow eyes ringed by shadow, scarlet locks tangled with sleep. A smile tugged at her lips.

A groan came from the opposite bed as Sam rolled over and pulled the pillow over his head.

"God," came Chris's voice from her other side.

Liz turned to face him. "What?"

He blinked and shook his head. "Your neck—no wonder you couldn't breathe. It's a rather attractive shade of purple."

Liz touched a finger to her throat, but flinched as the muscles spasmed. She bit her lip, swallowing the pain. "I've had worse."

She felt Chris shudder, but he said nothing.

For the next few minutes they sat in silence, listening to the growing crescendo of Sam's snores. Finally, Ashley stood and crossed to his bed. Taking a hold of his blanket, she tore it away, exposing his half-naked body to the cold. His curses echoed from the walls as Ashley retreated to her bed, bringing Sam's cover with her.

Liz chuckled as Ashley spread the cover over them, trying to ignore the burning from her throat. "Thanks, I was getting cold," she said, grinning at the other girl.

"Hey!" Sam was sitting up now, blinking hard in the fluorescent light. He tossed his pillow across the room. Chris caught it easily and placed it behind his head.

Liz smiled as a little of the weight lifted from her heart. Wriggling her backside, she snuggled in beneath the blanket, basking in the warm bodies to either side of her. They grinned as Sam found his shirt from the night before and pulled it over his broad shoulders. Liz watched with a tinge of disappointment as he covered himself.

"Hey, my eyes are up here, ladies," Sam laughed.

Liz snorted. "Like I'd be interested in a city slugger like you, Sam."

Ashley and Chris chuckled while Sam rolled his eyes. Then the clang of the outer door echoed down the corridor, plunging the room into silence. The smiles fell from their faces as they shared sad glances, the weight of yesterday's guilt returning.

"What happens next?" Chris murmured.

Sam's eyes flickered towards Ashley. "After we… survived, you two showed up," Sam replied with a shrug. "You know the rest."

Beside her, Ashley shifted on the bed. "Yesterday, on the training field, the doctors were talking," she said in a low voice. "I overheard a bit. They were talking about things moving ahead. So who knows what comes next?"

The bed shifted again as Chris pulled himself up. A pang of sadness touched Liz as his warmth left her side. He moved to the bars and glanced down the corridor. "Well, whatever comes next, at least breakfast is on its way." He spoke the words with a false lightness, failing to hide the strain beneath, but Liz appreciated his attempt to brighten the gloomy discussion.

Sam groaned. "Don't suppose it's something other than that gruel they call oatmeal?"

"Sure, what's your order? I'll give them a shout." Chris laughed.

"I'll take some eggs with a side of bacon. Maybe some hash browns. Oh, and a burger. You got all that?"

"How about a television while you're at it, Chris?" Ashley added.

Shaking his head, Chris returned to the bed and slid in beside Liz. "Ah, bacon. I can't even remember the last time we had that at home."

As his warmth returned Liz found herself sliding closer, until her side pressed up against him. A tingle ran up her arm at the touch, and she held her breath, waiting for him to pull away. When he didn't move, she smiled, only then recalling his comment about the bacon. Her grin spread. While the food on the ranch had not technically been theirs to eat, her family had made an art of pilfering extra supplies whenever they were available. Bacon had been just one of the many luxury food items she'd enjoyed.

"Oh, I don't know, back on the farm we had bacon and eggs for breakfast most days. It gets a little old."

She laughed as the three of them turned to stare at her. Unfortunately, her mirth was too much for her throat, and she broke into a coughing fit. It was a few minutes before she found her voice again.

"Country secret," she croaked at last, and the others groaned.

The screeching wheels of the breakfast cart came to a halt outside their cell. The guard banged his rifle against the bars while the other opened the grate through which they passed the food.

"Come and get it." The guard with the gun laughed. "Big day for you, I hear."

Chris retrieved the four bowls of oatmeal, much to Sam's chagrin, and they sat down to their meal.

Afterwards, the four of them lay back and waited, listening for the sound of the outer door. Closing her eyes, Liz did her best to ignore the agony that was her neck. Her good mood quickly fell away as the pain beat down on her. Silently, she cursed the doctors, the guards and their guns, even poor, dead Joshua for his vicious attack.

"What do you think that guard meant?" Sam asked after an hour, addressing what they had all been wondering at.

"Nothing good," Chris offered unhelpfully.

"Well, they need us alive for something," Ashley put in. She had joined Sam on the other bed now, surrendering her bed to Liz and Chris. "Whatever this place is, it's top secret. My parents weren't the most connected of individuals in the government, but most things reached the rumor mill at some point. I don't think this place was ever mentioned. As far as the media are concerned, the children of traitors were..." Her voice trailed off, and Liz felt a pang of sadness for the girl.

Without speaking, Sam reached up and placed an arm around Ashley, drawing her into a hug. Watching them, Liz's sadness grew, rising from some lonely chasm inside her. The last two years had been long and hard, and more than once she had found herself craving the touch of another human being. Licking her lips, she glanced at Chris, then gave herself a silent shake. Drawing up her knees, she hugged them to her chest.

Movement came from beside her, but it was just Chris rearranging himself on the bed. He spoke into the uncomfortable silence. "Maybe it's the same with our families then. Maybe they've been taken someplace else." There was no mistaking the tremor of hope in his voice.

As the others nodded, Liz closed her eyes. The others might still cling to the thought their families lived, but there was no such hope for hers.

"Wouldn't that be nice?" Sam replied with false cheer. "We can all have a reunion someday, share torture stories around the campfire—"

"Shut up, Sam." Ashley pushed him away and looked at Chris. "We can only hope, Chris. Although my sister…" She bowed her head, eyes shining. "She got in the way. They never gave her a chance."

Before any of them could respond, a loud clang echoed down the corridor.

The four of them exchanged a long glance.

"Showtime," Sam whispered.

❧ 21 ☙

The screech of iron rollers carried down the corridor as a cell door slid open. Liz and the others jumped from their beds and pressed themselves up against the bars. Head hard against the cold steel, Liz strained for a glimpse of what was happening. The faces of their fellow inmates appeared behind the bars of the other cells.

At the very limits of her view, Liz could just make out a group of doctors talking quietly around the cell at the end of the corridor. Beside them, guards were shouting at the occupants. They carried steel batons now, instead of the familiar rifles of the past few days.

The guards disappeared into the cell. The raised voices of the prisoners echoed down to them, followed by the muffled thud of steel on flesh.

Retreating from the bars, Liz looked at the

others. Sam and Chris stared back, their eyes wide, uncertainty written across their faces. Ashley only pursed her lips, her gaze roaming the cell.

Liz returned to the bars as a girl's cry echoed down the corridor. She watched the doctors gathering around a steel trolley. One was leaning over an open drawer on the side of the cart. Reaching inside, he drew out a packet of syringes. Vials of a clear liquid followed, which he handed out to the other doctors. Together, they turned and followed the guards into the cell. Another shriek echoed down the corridor, a boy's this time.

"What's going on?" Chris asked from behind her.

Liz glanced at the others. "It's some sort of injection. They've got syringes and a trolley loaded with God only knows what else."

As she finished speaking, a long, drawn-out scream erupted from the cell at the end of the corridor. Liz flinched, pressing her face hard against the bars. Distantly she remembered the faces of the two captives in that cell: a young girl with blonde hair, a boy with dreadlocks.

The girl's scream slowly faded, but before it ceased the boy's voice joined in, carrying the awful notes of agony to their little cell. Liz shuddered, fighting the urge to cover her ears. The shrieks rose and fell, twisting and cracking, almost inhuman in their anguish.

Turning, she saw the blood draining from the

other's faces, felt her own cheeks grow cold with a terrible fear.

Finally the screams died away, leaving only silence.

The screech of trolley wheels on concrete followed as the doctors made their way to the next cell.

"What do we do?" Chris asked again.

"We fight," came Ashley's reply.

Liz turned and stared at the girl, her heart thudding hard in her chest. "*What?*" From down the corridor came the rattle of another cell opening. "What about the collars—?" She broke off as a cough tore at her throat.

Staggering past the others, she fumbled at the sink and turned the faucet. As she drank, Ashley continued: "Those batons, why do they need them?" Her voice was calm now. "They haven't needed them until now."

"It's like you said before," Sam mused. "They don't want us dead. They've been saving us for something. For *this.*"

"Really?" Chris snapped. "Because I'm pretty sure they just killed those two."

"They're not using the collars," Liz croaked as she re-joined them. The realization had come as she pressed her mouth to the faucet, making the collar dig into her neck. "No guns *or* collars."

Sam grinned and cracked his knuckles. "In that case, I agree with Ashley."

Liz leaned against the pole of her bunk bed, drawing reassurance from its solidity. She looked at the others, her stomach fluttering. Sam looked more alive than she'd ever seen him, his eyes alight with a frightening rage. Chris stood beside him, tense and ready, one eye on the door to the cell.

And Ashley...just looked like Ashley—cool, calm, collected. She pushed past the boys as another scream rattled from the walls. As Liz and the others took up station near the door, Ashley crouched between the beds and lifted a piece of railing which lay wedged against the wall. Liz blinked, realizing it was the broken safety railing for her bed.

Ashley offered Sam the bar. Teeth flashing in a grin, he took it and held it up to the light. The three parts of the rail formed a distorted U-shape, with two short pieces of steel jutting from the longer center piece.

"Work at the joints, see if you can break them apart," Ashley said.

As Sam set to work trying to separate the bars, Ashley moved to the front of the cell and resumed her watch. Liz joined her, and together they followed their captors' slow progress through the prison.

"They're done with us," Chris whispered behind them.

Outside, the screams continued, at times fading, only to resume after the doctors entered the next cell.

"No," Ashley whispered. Her eyes took on a haunted look. "I think they're only just getting started."

"Here." Liz turned and Sam offered her one of the smaller bars. He grinned. "Just pretend they're city sluggers like me."

Liz smiled grimly. Silently, she reached out and squeezed his arm. He nodded and moved to Ashley and Chris, offering them the other two bars. Ashley took one, but Chris shook his head. His eyes did not leave the corridor, but he spoke from the side of his mouth.

"I'd prefer to keep my hands free, thanks."

Outside, the doctors had reached the cell directly across from them. Its only occupant stood at the bars, watching as the doctors drew to a halt outside. His eyes were bloodshot and tears streamed down his face.

"Please, I never did anything wrong." His voice was feeble, barely a whisper.

He retreated into his cell as the guards slid open the door. Before he could so much as raise his fists, they were on him, batons flashing in the fluorescent lights. A few seconds later they had him pinned to the bed. Without preamble, the doctors entered the cell. One pulled down the inmate's pants, while another prepared the needle. They gave him an injection into his buttocks, then the doctors and guards retreated from the cell, slamming the door closed behind them.

Liz flinched as the boy screamed and began to writhe. Then the guards stepped between them and the other cell, and there was no more time to consider their neighbor's plight.

Clenching her hand hard around her improvised weapon, Liz watched as the guards gathered near the door. The pain in her throat had strangely faded, leaving only a dull ache. Blood pounded in her ears as she tensed, readying herself.

"Stand back, drop those," one of the guards ordered, eyeing their makeshift batons.

When they didn't move, he turned to look at the doctors.

"What are you waiting for?" Doctor Radly's voice carried into the cell. "Get in there and take those off them. You know we can't use the collars. We can't have any interference with their nervous system."

The guard nodded and reached out to unlock the door. The others gathered behind him, seven in total, their batons held ready.

A strange calm settled over Liz as the door slid open, the terror of the past few days falling away. This was it. This was their only chance. If they failed, she knew in her heart they were lost.

As the first of the guards moved into the cell,

movement flickered beside Liz. She turned in time to see Chris lunge forward. The guard grinned and raised his baton, but Chris was faster still. Leaping lightly from the concrete floor, he twisted in the air to avoid the guard's blow, and then drove his boot into the side of the man's head.

Liz gaped as the man's eyes rolled up in his skull and he collapsed to the ground.

Chris landed lightly in the doorway and retreated to re-join them.

"Six to go." He grinned, his smile infectious.

Shaking her head, Liz gripped the metal bar tighter and tried to hide her shock.

Outside, the remaining guards grabbed their fallen comrade by the feet and dragged his unconscious body out into the corridor. One of the doctors crouched beside him and placed a stethoscope to his chest. Radly glanced down at the man, then back at the guards. Each of them dwarfed even Sam's large frame, but still they stood, hesitating in the hallway.

"Well?" Radly snapped. "What are we paying you for? Get in there!"

The guards shared a glance, then approached together. Pushing the sliding door wide open, they entered as a group this time. They paused for a second in the entryway, hefting their batons, then rushed forward.

Liz tensed as a guard came at her, his baton flashing for her face. She ducked, and the hackles on her neck tingled as it whistled over her head. Then she lifted her own weapon and drove it into the man's midriff.

The blow caught him as he was moving forward, and his own weight drove the air from his lungs. Liz lifted her bar to strike him again, then threw herself to the side as another guard swung at her. The clang of steel rang out as the baton left a dent in the bunk bed behind her.

Recovering, she turned and found the first guard already straightening. The two of them bore down on her, forcing her away from the others.

Liz gripped her makeshift weapon tight, knowing she was hopelessly outmatched. Snarling, she threw herself forward anyway. They grinned, raised their batons. Then another guard staggered into them, sending them stumbling forward. Seeing her chance, Liz swung her pole into the face of the nearest guard.

There was a satisfying *crunch* as her baton struck home, and he dropped without a sound. She leapt for the gap he'd left, trying to re-join the others, but the second guard had already recovered. He stepped in to block her, his baton already in motion. The blow caught her in the stomach, knocking the breath from her lungs and sending her backwards into the wall.

Groaning, she tried to recover, but a fist caught her in the side of the face. Her feet crumpled beneath the force of the blow, and she slid sideways into the crook between the wall and the bunk.

Tasting blood in her mouth, she tried to get her hands and knees beneath her, but a heavy boot crashed into her back, pinning her down.

Her ears ringing, Liz twisted, desperate for a glimpse of the others. But the fight was already over. In the narrow confines, the guards' weight and numbers had made short work of the four prisoners. Sam lay immobilized on his own bed, one arm twisted behind his back and a guard's knee pressed between his shoulder blades. Ashley was similarly restrained on the floor nearby, while Chris still stood, his arms held by a man on either side of him. The last guard was just getting to his feet, a nasty bruise on his forehead.

"About time," Radly's sarcastic voice came from somewhere out of view. "Would you like something easier next time? Maybe some toddlers?"

The guards were silent as the doctors filed in, carrying an assortment of vials and syringes. As the doctors prepared themselves, Radly looked around the room. His eyes settled on Liz. "Get her up."

Tears stung Liz's eyes as a rough hand grasped a handful of her hair and pulled. Screaming, she drove a fist into the man's side, but the blow hardly seemed to faze him. A sharp pain came from her scalp as he pulled again. Kicking and screaming, Liz was hauled to her feet.

"This one's feisty," the guard commented as he tossed her onto Ashley's bed.

Before Liz could free herself, a guard landed on her back. An awful helplessness welled in her as she tried and failed to shift his weight. Pain lanced from her scalp again as the guard yanked her head back, forcing her to look at them.

"Stay still," he growled in her ear.

"Please don't do this," Ashley pleaded from the floor.

The thud of a boot striking flesh silenced her desperate words. A low groan followed. Liz twisted again, trying to get a glimpse of her friend, but the white coat of a doctor moved to block her view. Doctor Radly stared down at her.

"Enough," Radly said, his tone brooking no argument.

Unlike Halt, Radly did not appear to take any joy in their pain. Rather, he didn't seem to care about their comfort one way or another. He moved around the cell with a cold efficiency, retrieving a stoppered vial from the hands of another doctor. Lifting a nasty-looking syringe, he eyed the thick needle for a second before driving it through the vial's rubber stopper. Then he drew back the plunger and the liquid disappeared into the syringe.

"Doctor Faulks," Radly said, addressing someone standing just outside of Liz's view, "this is the PERV-A strain?"

"Yes," a woman's reply came quickly. "We've

already finished with the B strain. The rest are marked down for PERV-A."

Nodding, Radly turned back to Liz. "Hold her." Liz shuddered as the guard shifted, taking a firmer grip of her shoulders.

From the corner of her eye, she watched Radly approach, his gloved hands cradling the syringe. He disappeared from her line of vision. Seconds later, firm hands tugged at her pants, and a cold breeze blew across her backside. She tensed, pushing back against her assailant's relentless strength.

A sigh came from behind her. "This will go easier for you if you relax, Ms. Flores."

Hearing her last name sent a bolt of shock through Liz. For a second she hesitated, then bit off a string a profanity that would have made even her father blush.

Another sigh, then a cold cloth pressed against her butt-cheek. A shiver raced up her spine, more shock from the violation than from the cold. A low, guttural growl built in her throat, and the guard's knee pressed harder into the small of her back. She no longer cared. A desperate horror was growing within her, an awful fear, a need to break free.

She screamed again, writhing and bucking beneath the guard, straining to shift his weight.

A sudden pinch came from her naked backside, followed by a strange pressure that spread quickly across her cheek. It was gentle at first, a cold numbness that tingled as it went. But it warmed quickly, like a fire gathering heat, until her muscles were aflame from its touch. The tingling raced outwards, spreading to her legs and back.

Liz gasped, fighting the pain, desperate to fend it off. She gritted her teeth, tensing against its relentless spread. The pressure on her back vanished as the guard released her, but by then she barely noticed. Her attention was elsewhere, her focus fixed on the sensations rippling through her body.

Then, as though a switch had been flicked, the muscles down the length of her back locked in a sudden cramp. Pain unlike any Liz had experienced closed around her, walling her off from the world, trapping her in the fiery arms of its cage. Her eyes snapped open, but all she saw were stars, whirling across her vision, blinding in their brilliance. In the distance she heard a scream, a girl's voice tearing at the blackness of her mind, but she could do nothing to help her now.

Agony engulfed her body, her mind, her very soul.

III

REBIRTH

❦ 22 ❦

C*old.*
    The thought filtered through the thick sludge of Chris's mind, parting the darkness like a curtain. Then it was all around him, wrapping his body in an icy blanket, turning his breath to ragged gasps. A shiver caught him, rippling down his body, throwing off the last dregs of sleep.

Frozen air burned his nostrils as he inhaled, bringing with it the familiar tang of bleach. But there was more to the scent now, an underlying stench of rot and decay that made his stomach swirl. Opening his mouth, he tasted the metallic reek of blood and vomit.

Sound was the next sense to return. His ears tingled, catching the murmur of a breath, the creak of metal joints moving beneath restless bodies, the hiss of an air conditioner. From somewhere in the room came the whisper of machines, the familiar whine of overhead lights.

I'm alive. The words whispered in Chris's mind, though he couldn't quite recall why that surprised him.

Keeping his eyes closed, he sucked in another breath, struggling to restore the shattered pieces of his consciousness. Dimly he remembered the fire burning up his spine, spreading to his chest, filling his lungs. But there was no pain now, only the dull ache of his muscles, as though they had lain unused for countless days.

How long? His brow creased.

How long had he lain here, unconscious, in the clutches of whatever drug the doctors had given him?

Sounds came from all around him, growing louder, echoing as though from a wide expanse. Chains rattled as he moved his arms, and he felt the cold touch of steel restraining his wrists. Without opening his eyes, Chris knew he'd been handcuffed to the bed.

Apparently, the doctors weren't taking any chances with their patients.

Memories drifted through the darkness of his thoughts, rising as though from a fog. Images of the fight flashed by, the *crack* as Sam fell to a baton, the *thud* of Ashley hitting the floor. He had not seen what happened to Liz, not until the guards had overwhelmed him, and he'd found her curled up in the corner.

Helpless, he had watched as they'd lifted Liz onto the bed and injected her with something. Her screams had been instant and horrifying, so deafening that even the guards had retreated from her. Her agony tore at his soul, begged for him to save her from the monsters. But he had been powerless against the raw strength of the men on either side of him.

His heart beat harder at the memory. A sense of urgency took him, and he shifted his arms, testing the movement allowed by the handcuffs. The links rattled as he ran a hand along the chain and found where they attached to the bed's guardrail.

Other sounds came to him now: the beeping of a nearby machine, the whir of a pump, the hiss of air escaping tubes. His breath quickened, and he heard the beeping accelerate, matching the racing of his heart.

Somewhere in the room, a door banged. Chris froze, his fingers still clenched around the metal bar. The soft tread of footsteps crossed the room, followed by voices.

"Has the danger passed?" Halt's voice came from Chris's right.

"We think so." Chris recognized Fallow, though her voice was strained, exhausted. "It was a close thing though. I *told* you it wasn't ready."

"Perhaps," Halt replied, "but we expected losses. Despite our best efforts, some of the candidates were simply too weak to withstand the morphological alterations."

"We lost forty percent!" Chris winced as Fallow's voice cracked. He heard a sharp exhalation of breath, before she continued in a calmer voice. "I expected mortality to be less than fifteen. As it is, we barely have a viable population. If we'd had more time…"

"More time?" Halt laughed. "That is the cry of a coward, Fallow! More time, more money, always more *something!*" He took a breath. "As Archimedes once said: 'Give me a lever and a place to stand, and I will move the earth.' But us mere mortals only have the time and resources the government has provided us. And our time is up."

"The *government* will not be satisfied with a forty percent mortality rate, Halt," Fallow growled.

"No," came the head doctor's swift reply, "but if the survivors show promise, you will have won the time you need to find perfection, Fallow."

Silence followed. Slowly their footsteps came closer. Listening to the beep of the machine beside him, Chris held his breath, struggling to slow his racing heart.

"And have we succeeded, Fallow?" Halt's voice was eager.

It was a while before the woman replied. "The

results are mixed. Tissue samples taken over the last few weeks show a steady integration between the host chromosomes and the viral DNA. Candidates who received the PERV-A strain have advanced more rapidly than PERV-B, and now show complete integration. However, we have yet to determine whether the altered genomes are expressing correctly."

"Excellent." There was unmasked glee in Halt's voice. "When do you expect they'll be ready to test genome expression?"

"We've taken them off the immunosuppressants. So far they've shown no adverse reactions. We expect them to wake from their comas over the next few days. Once they're conscious, we can begin testing their basic motor skills and cognitive function, to determine whether the virus had any degenerative effects…" Fallow trailed off as Halt snorted.

"We don't have time to waste on your procedures, Fallow. We need to move onto the second phase. For that we need *results*."

"I don't see how—" Fallow began.

"Don't give me that, Fallow," Halt snapped. "You know very well there is no need for your tests. As far as the Director is concerned, there is only one test the candidates need to pass."

There was a long pause before Fallow replied. "Halt…" Her voice was entreating now. "That's simply not possible. They've been unconscious for weeks. The recovery time alone…they're in no condition—"

"If the experiment succeeded, recovery time should not be an issue." Halt's voice sounded like he was just a few feet away now. "Look, this one appears to be conscious."

A tingle raced up Chris's spine at the man's words. Silently he fought the instinct to leap from the bed and flee. His arms prickled as goosebumps spread along his skin.

"You're right." Fallow's murmur seemed to come from directly overhead. "Her heartbeat has recovered to normal levels."

A girl's cry came from nearby, followed by the angry rattle of chains. Chris cracked his eyes open a fraction, desperate to see what was happening. Pain shot through his skull as white light streamed between his eyelids, momentary blinding him. Then the light faded and the room clicked into focus. Rows of beds stretched across a wide room, each occupied by an unconscious patients dressed in green gowns. A tangle of tubes and wires covered each body like a spiderweb spun around a fly. From the brief glimpse he caught, Chris guessed there were some seventy beds, though many were empty.

The girl Halt and Fallow were discussing was sitting up in the hospital bed directly across from Chris. Her back was turned to him, and both her arms were chained to the railings. Curly black hair tumbled around her shoulders, and with a shiver of recognition, Chris realized it was Liz.

She's alive!

Chris struggled to muffle his sharp intake of breath. Beside him, the beeping of the machine started to race. He clenched the sidebar of his bed until his palms hurt. Through the shadows of his eyelashes, he watched Halt move to stand over Liz.

"Incredible." Halt was studying the machine beside Liz's bed. Lines and numbers flashed across the screen, Chris guessed providing readings from the tubes and wires that covered Liz. "Look at her vitals."

Fallow stood in silence beside him, shadows ringing her eyes, her lips pursed tight.

Halt shook his head. "I would say she is fully recovered, wouldn't you, Doctor Fallow?"

Reluctantly Fallow nodded, a look of resignation coming over her face.

"Excellent, then I see no reason to delay. Get her ready."

Blood pounded in Chris's head, drowning out all reason. He didn't know what Halt had planned for Liz, what fresh horrors awaited her, but he refused to lie quietly while she faced it alone. Whatever happened, they were still in this together. For all he knew, Sam and Ashley might already be gone, but Liz still lived. He would not lose her now.

"Leave her alone," he growled, sitting up in the bed.

Liz turned towards him, her eyes widening with shock. Behind her, Fallow's face seemed to crumple, while a grin spread slowly across Halt's face. In that instant, Chris felt a pit open in his stomach; a sudden realization he had made a terrible mistake.

Still, it was worth it to see the relief sweep across Liz's face.

"Excellent." Halt clapped his hands. "Bring him, too. It may even the odds."

23

Liz shivered as Fallow unlocked the cuffs around her wrists. Blinking, she looked at the woman's face. Her features faded in and out of focus. A wave of nausea swept through Liz's stomach, and she had to clench the sidebar to steady herself.

"Are you okay?" Fallow asked.

Liz flinched as a hand touched her shoulder. "*Don't!*" she growled, leaning back.

Closing her eyes, Liz willed her stomach to settle, then opened them again. To her relief, the features of Fallow's face finally snapped into place. She blinked again, surprised to see the dark rings beneath the woman's eyes, the patchwork of tiny cracks across the skin of her cheeks, the thin red capillaries threading her eyes. Her head swam; she had never noticed so much detail in a person's face before.

"I'm sorry." Liz's ears twitched at the sound, before a harsh shriek cut through the words.

She recoiled, slapping her hands over her ears. Distantly she heard the doctor's voice over the ringing. A hand reached for her, but she twisted, falling sideways on the bed. Fallow paused, staring down at her, and then retreated a step.

Slowly the ringing died away, and Liz finally removed her hands from her ears.

"I'm sorry." Fallow's voice was a whisper now, but Liz heard it with perfect clarity. "How do you feel?"

Gritting her teeth, Liz glanced across at Chris. As their eyes met her heart lurched, and she felt again the relief that had swept through her when he'd sat up.

He's alive!

Despite the apparent odds against them, the two of them had survived whatever demented experiment the doctors had performed on them. Beside her, Fallow was removing the various tubes and wires that linked Liz to the machine.

"Why are you doing this?" Liz tried and failed to keep the loathing from her voice.

Fallow sighed, her eyes flickering away. "You'll find out soon enough, Elizabeth."

Liz stared at the grief shining from Fallow's eyes. Despite herself, she found herself pitying the woman, though she could not say why. Even so, the doctor's words triggered a sense of foreboding, and Liz pressed on, desperate to exploit the woman's weakness.

"You don't have to do this," she whispered. "Halt's gone. You could let us go, unlock our collars."

A faint smile twitched on Fallow's lips. "A tempting proposition." She shook her head. "They'd kill you both before you reached the front door. And then they'd come for me." Their eyes locked, but after a moment Fallow only smiled and continued with false humor. "Besides, you are the culmination of my life's work."

"What about *our* lives?" Chris's snarl came from behind Liz. "What right—?"

He broke off as Fallow raised a hand, her smile fading. "You know the law, Christopher. Your mother was found guilty of treason. In due time, she will answer for those crimes. As her son, you would have faced the same fate."

To Liz, Fallow's words sounded hollow, as though they left a bad taste in her mouth. Even so, after that the woman ignored their pleas. Moving to Chris, she removed the cuffs and wires. Within a few minutes she had them on their feet, dressed in fresh orange jumpsuits, and staggering around the room like senior citizens.

Liz's legs trembled with each step, refusing to obey the simplest of instructions. A dull ache was quickly spreading up her hamstrings, and several times she had to grab at neighboring beds to steady herself. Chris was no better; he managed to knock over a series of machines within two steps of leaving his bed, after which he promptly crashed to the linoleum floor.

From the corner of her eyes, Liz caught movement from several of the beds, but the doctor was too preoccupied with Chris to notice. Steadying herself, she took a moment to search the room for Ashley and Sam. But the fluorescent light caught in her eyes, and she found her vision shimmering, the room becoming a blur. By the time it cleared, Fallow was already shepherding them towards the doorway.

Outside, Liz's legs finally started to obey, though they remained stiff and sore. Chris was steadily improving too, but he still needed Liz's shoulder for support. Two guards stood on either side of exit, but neither made any move to follow them. Fallow kept pace several feet behind them though, no doubt ready to use the collars should they place a foot out of line.

Step by faltering step, they made their way through the facility, obeying Fallow's direction whenever they came to an intersection. Within a few turns, Chris had recovered enough to walk unaided, though it was a while before he managed more than a slow shuffling. Fortunately, the doctor did not seem to be in any hurry.

Despite their slow pace, the journey could not last forever, and all too soon they found themselves outside a familiar white door. Liz shivered as she looked on it, memories of her fight with Joshua spiraling through her mind.

She turned as Fallow spoke from behind them. "Go in."

Wordlessly, Liz shook her head. Dread wrapped around her stomach as she reached out and took Chris's hand. Together they faced the doctor, standing straight now, the strength slowly returning to their limbs.

"We won't." Liz drew herself up and stepped towards Fallow. "I won't."

Fallow retreated. She lifted her arm, the watch on her wrist flashing in warning. "Won't what?" Fallow asked.

"I won't fight her," Chris coughed. "I'd rather die."

Fallow's shoulders slumped and she gave a little shake of her head. "That's not…no." She gestured with a hand. "Just go."

Liz and Chris shared a glance, still hesitating. Despite Fallow's strange reassurance, fear gnawed at Liz's stomach, a dread she could not shake. The last time she'd entered this room, an innocent boy had lost his life. She had almost lost her own. Her hand drifted to her throat, but there was no pain now, only the cold reminder of the collar nestled beneath her chin.

How long were we asleep?

"Don't make me use the collars." Fallow lifted her finger to her watch.

They went.

As the door clicked shut behind them, Liz found herself standing again in the padded room, blinking in the brilliant light. An awful smell wafted through the air, a sickly sweetness that clung to her nostrils. As her vision cleared and the room came into focus, she realized with a sharp inhalation that they were not alone.

A boy stood in the center of the room. He wore an orange jumpsuit that matched their own, though she had never seen him before in the cells. His head was bowed, and his breath came in ragged gasps, his shoulders trembling with each violent exhalation. He held his hands clenched at his side, and though his eyes were open, he did not seem to have noticed them. Black hair dangled in front of his face, obscuring the rest of his features.

Liz edged towards him, her heart beating hard in her chest. Behind her, Chris gasped, and she felt his hand on her shoulder. But she twisted free, her panic growing. Gripped by a desperate need to see, to know for sure, she slid closer.

Leaning down, she peered into the boy's eyes.

Hard grey irises stared back, their surfaces glazed, unseeing.

But as she watched, they blinked, the life behind them stirring.

Liz screamed.

❧ 24 ❧

Chris recognized what the boy was the instant they stepped into the room. Though there was no outward difference to his appearance, there was a strangeness to his hunched stance, something about how he stood that gave it away. The stench of him was strong in the room, a cloying sweetness that clung to the air.

He didn't need to see the grey eyes to know what the boy was.

Chead.

He had tried to stop Liz, but she'd only shaken herself free and crept closer. Clenching his fists, he tested his strength, surprised by how quickly it was returning. His attention was drawn back to Liz as she bent down to peer into the boy's face.

Then she was staggering backwards, her scream

reverberating around the room. The *Chead's* features contorted, the ripple of awakening sweeping across its face, and then Chris was retreating too, fumbling at the door, shouting for help, knowing it would not come.

Beside him, Liz screamed again and staggered sideways. Chris's hand flashed out, catching her sleeve and dragging her back to him. She started to thrash, and her panic swept through him, waking him from his stupor. He shoved Liz behind him and faced the *Chead*.

He froze as he found the iron-grey eyes watching him. A smile spread across the creature's face, sending pure terror sizzling through every fiber of Chris's being. Another shriek came from behind him as Liz pounded on the padded door.

Taking a breath, Chris stepped towards the *Chead*, an eerie calm coming over him. He placed himself squarely between Liz and the creature, ignoring the urge to turn and shake her, to pull her back from the edge. Liz's words were still fresh in his mind, and he heard again the agony in her voice as she'd told him of her parents' death at the hands of a *Chead*.

He couldn't blame her for panicking.

Chris stared into the eyes of the *Chead*, searching for a sign of sanity, for a hint of the human it had once been.

The *Chead* raised an eyebrow. "Welcome," it whispered, the word sounding strange from its mouth, robotic, as though speech did not come easily to it.

For a second all Chris could do was stand and gape. He blinked, moving his mouth, struggling to find the words. "Wha…what?" he finally managed.

Grey eyes flickered from Chris to Liz. With deliberate slowness, the *Chead* turned and began to pace. It walked first towards the mirror, pausing as its reflection rose up before it, a snarl twisting its lips. Then it spun, moving back past Chris and Liz until it reached the far wall. A growl rumbled from its chest as it turned and repeated the maneuver, its jerky movements like those of a caged animal. Metal shone around its neck, and for the first time Chris realized it too was wearing a collar.

"What. Am. I?" The creature ground out the words. It paused and looked straight at Chris. "You already know that…"

Chris did not reply. His mind was still reeling, struggling to comprehend one irresolvable revelation: it could speak—not just that, it understood him. No newspaper, no television channel had ever mentioned a *Chead* speaking, never mind being self-aware. As far as the public were concerned, the things were monsters—uncontrollable, terrible, killing machines.

They did not think.

They certainly did not talk.

"How?" Chris croaked.

He could sense Liz behind him regaining her composure. The thuds on the door had ceased, her screams dying to soft gasps. On trembling legs, Liz stumbled forward to join him. Out of the corner of his eye, he watched a shiver run through her and reached out an arm. Their hands touched, their fingers entwining. He gave her hand a squeeze and turned back to the *Chead*.

It had stopped its pacing and stood again in the center of the room, watching them. Its nostrils flared as it inhaled.

"You smell…different," it said, then: "How do I speak?" It spoke Chris's question aloud.

Chris nodded his confirmation.

A smile spread across the *Chead's* face. "I learned." It nodded towards the mirror. "From them…"

Liz's hand shook in Chris's grip, but when he looked at her, Liz's eyes remained fixed straight ahead, her lips pressed tightly together.

The *Chead's* head bent to the side, as though in curiosity. "You are different," it said again, its smile spreading, though there was no humor in its eyes. "Like me."

Chris's stomach clenched at its words. "What do you mean? We're…we're not like you…" he croaked.

An awful laughter crackled up from the thing's

throat. "They succeeded…these jailers of ours." The boy's face twisted horribly, until it seemed some demon now possessed the boy. Speech seemed to come easier to it now. "But I wonder, is it enough?"

It stepped towards them then, the grin fading.

As one, Chris and Liz retreated across the padded floor, until their backs were pressed against the door.

Chris raised his hands in surrender. "Please, wait, you don't have to do this."

The *Chead* paused, the hard glint in its eyes wavering. It shook its head. "But I do. It is my nature…isn't it?" It took another step, its eyes flickering to the one-way glass. "Besides, it's what *they* want."

Snarling, the *Chead* leapt towards them.

Without pausing to think, Chris pushed Liz from him and stepped in to meet the creature's charge. From the corner of his eye he saw Liz stagger sideways. Then the *Chead* was on him, its fist flashing for his chest. Acting on instinct drilled into him by years of Taekwondo, he threw up an arm, and the blow glanced from his forearm.

Chris gasped as pain jolted his wrist. Then the weight of the creature crashed into him, flinging him backwards into the wall. The *Chead* was on Chris before he could recover, catching him by the shoulders. His stomach twisted as the long arms lifted him.

Panicked, he kicked out, driving a desperate blow into the boy's head.

To his surprise, the *Chead* reeled back. A savage growl came from its throat as it tossed him aside. Chris bent his head and braced his arms as the ground raced towards him. He struck with a thud and rolled, spinning to come to his feet in one fluid movement. Straightening, he faced the *Chead*.

The creature stared back, watching him like a predator stalking its prey. Slowly it lifted an arm and wiped a trickle of blood from its lip.

Chris's gaze flickered as he caught sight of Liz. She moved to join him, her eyes flashing. "Don't do that again," she growled.

Nodding, Chris turned his attention back to the *Chead*. It seemed hesitant now. Chris was glad for its caution. On the television, he'd watched a *Chead* tear men apart, seen throats ripped out and skulls shattered by a single blow. Tasers did little to slow them, and bullets only seemed to anger them unless they struck something vital.

Unarmed and trapped in the tiny room, Chris did not like their odds.

Yet somehow, his blow had rattled it.

Pushing down his fear, Chris edged away from Liz. Whatever their chances, they had to try. At least they outnumbered the *Chead*. They needed to make the most of that advantage.

The *Chead* snarled as he moved, its head turning

to follow him. Chris watched as Liz edged sideways in the opposite direction. The *Chead* ignored her though, clearly seeing Chris as the greater threat.

Chris just hoped Liz had the strength to prove it wrong.

The *Chead's* grin returned as Chris came to a stop. A low rumble quivered in its chest. It stepped towards him, legs tensing to spring. Chris raised his fists in reply. Sliding one leg backwards, he twisted sideways, planting himself in a defensive stance. Flashing a grin he did not feel, he gestured the creature forward.

As Chris hoped, his impudence ignited a flash of anger in the *Chead*. Adrenaline pounded in his ears as it charged, and he reacted without thought, years of training taking over. One hand swept up to deflect a blow flashing for his face. The force of the attack sent him reeling, but stepping back he managed to keep his balance, already watching for the next attack.

Another fist came at his face and he ducked. His surprise grew as the attack flew past. He'd seen a *Chead* shatter bones with a single blow. By all rights, Chris's arm should have been crushed. Yet somehow he was holding his own.

The *Chead* seemed to have realized this too. Snarling, it hurled itself at Chris with renewed fury. A fist flashed beneath his guard and struck him in the stomach. The breath hissed between Chris's teeth as his lungs emptied. Wheezing, he tried to retreat, but the Chead was too close.

With a shriek, Liz leapt into the fray. Bent in two and gasping, Chris caught a glimpse of her tangled hair and flashing blue eyes as she drove her foot down into the back of the *Chead's* knee.

Screaming, it collapsed.

🙦 25 🙤

The second Liz had seen the stone-grey eyes of the *Chead*, the memories came flooding back, and she'd found herself back in her parents' house, in the home she'd been raised in. Once, it had been a safe place, a sanctuary amidst the harsh world outside.

Now though, in her memories, a perpetual shadow hung over its wooden hallways, sucking away the light, the life it had once born.

In her mind, she saw again the rubble-strewn corridor, the broken floorboards and pooling blood. She saw herself turn the corner, saw the body lying in the corridor, strangely whole, while those outside had lain in pieces.

And her mother, standing over the body, her grey eyes staring.

With a scream, Liz tore herself from the memory, returning to the present, to the room, and to Chris.

And to the *Chead*.

Still reeling, caught in the clutches of remembered horror, she'd barely heard the conversation between Chris and the *Chead*. She had only woken when Chris had pushed her from the path of *Chead's* charge. Anger had lit in her stomach, waking her from the fear, restoring her to life.

Now, as she edged sideways around the *Chead*, she let that anger grow, fed it with every injustice she'd ever suffered. It was her only weapon now, her only strength against the sheer ferocity of the creature standing between them. Opposite her, Chris faced the creature, drawing it away, until its back was turned to her. But before she could strike, the *Chead* leapt for Chris.

Fear chilled her stomach as blows crashed against flesh. To her surprise, Chris did not go down. Edging closer, she saw him deflect another blow, his arms moving faster than thought, the *crack* of fists connecting with bone ringing from the walls.

Liz stared, her mouth wide with disbelief. What she was watching was not possible. Chris was keeping pace with the violent speed of the *Chead*, matching it blow for blow, punch for punch. Her eyes could barely keep up with their frenzied movements. The air itself seemed to shake with the strength of each clash, and still Chris stood, holding his own.

What have they done to us?

Her skin tingled as the question whispered in her mind. But there was no time to contemplate the answers, no time to consider the implications. Instead, she gathered herself and slid closer, searching for an opening.

Then, an attack slipped beneath Chris's guard. It slammed into his stomach, driving him to his knees. The color fled his face as the *Chead* stepped in, raising a fist to deliver the final blow.

Seeing her chance, Liz sprang forward and drove her heel into the back of the *Chead's* knee. Idly, she hoped whatever changes had been wrought on the *Chead* had not removed the cluster of nerve endings located behind the kneecap.

The boy's bloodcurdling shriek answered her question. The *Chead's* leg crumbled beneath the force of the blow, sending it crashing to the ground. Clenching her teeth, Liz stepped towards it as Chris rolled away.

She swung a kick at its head, but the *Chead* was already recovering. Quick as a cobra it twisted, a hand flashing out to catch her by the leg. Before she could free herself, it stood, grey eyes glittering. A growl came from its throat as it lifted her by the leg and held her upside-down. Gasping, she fought to break its hold, but its fingers were like iron. Knowing it was useless, Liz lashed out with a fist, catching it in the cheek.

Shock reverberated up her arm as the blow connected. The fingers around her leg loosened, and suddenly she was falling. She landed awkwardly and looked up to see the *Chead* stumbling backwards, one hand raised to its face. It straightened with a roar, its gaze sweeping down to find her on the floor.

Liz's courage crumbled as she looked into its awful eyes. All semblance of humanity had fled the creature now, melting in the red-hot flames of its rage. Hardly daring to breathe, she backed towards Chris, any thoughts of attacking falling away.

Snarling, it stepped after her.

"Now you've done it," Chris panted, his hand reaching for hers.

She clenched her hand around his, drawing strength from his presence, then released him. Together they watched the *Chead* approach.

With a roar, it leapt.

Chris sprang forward to meet it, screaming his defiance. He deflected the first swing of the creature's fist, but this time the force of the blow sent him reeling, and Liz had to step aside to avoid him. Then the *Chead* was on her, fists flying, lips drawn back in a snarl, its half-mad screams echoing from the mirrored glass.

A fist caught Liz in the cheek, staggering her, then the *Chead's* shoulder crashed into her chest. The breath rushed from her lungs as she was thrown backwards into the wall. Her head whipped back, striking the padding, and despite the soft surface, her vision spun. Groaning, she slid down the wall, struggling to catch her breath.

Across the room, Chris fought on, but he was no longer a match for the *Chead's* strength. And it was faster now, its speed and ferocity far beyond human capabilities. With contempt, it knocked aside his blows. A fist crashed into his face, sending him stumbling backwards, but he refused to yield. Straightening, he launched himself back into the fray.

Desperately, Liz struggled back to her feet.

A shout drew her attention back to the fight. The *Chead* had caught Chris's fist in one hand. Chris screamed again, though this time neither of them moved. An awful *crack* came from Chris's fist as he sank to his knees. The color fled his face and he gave an awful groan. One-handed, he struggled to get his feet back under him—until the *Chead's* other hand smashed into the side of his head. Chris went limp at the blow, his breathing ragged, one hand still caught in the creature's grip.

Silently, Liz stood. The *Chead's* back was turned to her, its attention focused on tearing Chris limb from limb. She flinched as another blow thudded into Chris's head. This time he made no effort to avoid it. A low gurgle came from his throat as the *Chead* lifted him by the arm, dragging him back to his feet.

Liz moved quickly, knowing she only had seconds to act. The soft floor made no noise beneath her bare feet. Without pausing to think, she hurled herself at the creature's back. This time she aimed high, sweeping her forearm over its shoulder. Before it could react, she pulled her arm tight against its throat and leaned back. Her feet caught the ground and she pulled harder, dragging it backwards off-balance.

The *Chead* gave a strangled cry. Releasing Chris, it turned its attention on her. Knowing she could not match its strength or weight, Liz allowed herself to fall backwards, dragging the *Chead* down with her. It landed on her chest, driving the breath from her lungs, but still she held on, forearm tight across its collared throat.

Sensing its plight, the *Chead* thrashed against her. Its legs kicked out, catching Liz in the shins. Pain lanced from her leg as something went *crack*, but no force on earth would make her let go now.

Not even death.

Long seconds passed, and the creature's struggles weakened. Its legs no longer beat against the floor, and its relentless strength no longer pressed so hard against her.

Movement came from beyond the *Chead*. Chris staggered to his feet, his face already turning purple from bruises, one eye so swollen she could barely see it. Even so, he stumbled forward and fell to his knees beside her. Raising his fist, he drove it into the *Chead's* face.

Liz felt the power of Chris's blow through the *Chead*. Its body went limp in her arms, but still she did not relent.

Only when she was satisfied it was no longer moving did Liz loosen her grip. With Chris's help, they heaved the dead weight from her chest.

Then she was embracing Chris, pulling him to her, clinging desperately at his back. An awful sob built in her chest and escaped in a rush. Chris's arms tightened around her, and then he was sobbing too, his hot wet tears falling on her shoulder.

They clung to each other in silence, and let the horror wash over them.

❦ 26 ❦

C hris looked up as a click came from the doorway. Halt stood there, a triumphant grin stretching across his thin lips. His eyes feasted on the two of them, shining with a wild exaltation.

"It worked," he said, his voice raw. He stepped into the room, two guards following him before the door swung shut. "The genomes are expressing—a few at least. Muscle density factor, reaction time, agility, it's all there…"

As the man rambled, Chris struggled to pull his mind back to the present. He wrapped his arm around Liz, pulling her tight against him. She shivered and they shared a glance.

Then she turned, facing Halt. "What have you done to us?" she croaked.

Halt drew to a stop. He blinked, looking almost surprised, as though he had forgotten they could speak. His smile faded as he crossed his arms. "We have enhanced you, my dear. Made you better… made you *useful*." He almost spat the last word.

Chris met the man's iron gaze. "*Why?*" He gestured to the *Chead*. "Why would you do this? Send us in here to die?"

Halt stepped towards the unconscious *Chead*. "To see if you would live," he answered, looking back over his shoulder. "To see if we had succeeded in creating a weapon that could match the *Chead*."

Rage constricted Chris's chest at the doctor's words. He stared up at the man, struggling to breathe. Pain shot from his knuckles—where the *Chead* had held him—as he clenched his fists. Glancing at his hand, he saw it had already swollen to twice its usual size.

He shuddered.

It would have killed me.

"You changed us." Liz was speaking again, her voice barely audible. "Did something to us…while we slept. *How…why?*" Her voice cracked. She was shaking in his arms, though whether from rage or some other emotion, Chris could not tell.

Chuckling, Halt walked towards them. "It was a simple matter, in the end. A little retrovirus, some genetic mapping of various species—chimpanzees, wolves, felines, eagles, and so on. Isolating the desirable genes took time, as did altering their repetition sequences to be accepted by human cells." He shrugged. "But, well, the results were worth the effort. And the best is yet to come." An awful grin spread across his face.

With Halt's words, Chris mind finally caught up with events. Revulsion struck him as he realized the truth—that the *Chead* had not been weaker than those on the television. It was he and Liz who had changed. They were stronger.

And it was Fallow and Halt who had changed them.

A scream built in Chris's chest as he looked at the doctor. An awful sense of violation wrapped around his throat. He clenched his fist again, felt the pain, its sharpness anchoring him to reality. He felt defiled, like something had been taken from him, stolen. The pain built in his hand, but it was nothing to the desecration of his body. He drew back his lips in a snarl.

Halt watched them, his expression unchanged, but his hand drifted towards his watch. Tension hung in the air as Chris's rage gathered strength.

Then a groan came from across the room. Halt's eyes flickered towards the *Chead*. Chris followed his gaze and saw the creature had rolled onto its side. It moaned again, then started to cough. Its eyes fluttered but did not open.

"It's still alive." Halt sounded surprised. He turned back to Chris. "Kill it."

"What?" Chris blinked, staring at the doctor in disbelief.

"Kill it," Halt repeated. "That monstrosity is not worthy of this earth. Kill it, Christopher. Prove you are its superior."

"No." Chris was surprised by his own resolve. Releasing Liz, he faced Halt, determined to defy him. "I won't."

Halt shook his head and held up his arm. The watch flashed on his wrist. "Do not waste my time, Christopher. Kill the *Chead*, and we can move on from this unpleasant business."

A peal of laughter came from beside Chris, then Liz spoke. "No, Halt. We won't. We're not your creatures, your slaves to do with as you please. Whatever you've done to us, we're still human."

Halt did not move. His eyes flickered for a second to Liz, then back to Chris. "I will give you one last chance, Christopher. Kill the *Chead. Now!*"

"You're the monstrosity, Halt," Chris replied.

"Very well." Halt looked at Liz again. "If that is your decision…"

He pressed his finger to the watch.

Chris closed his eyes and braced himself for the pain. Sucking in a breath, he waited for the familiar fire to encircle his throat, to sap the strength from his legs, to lock his muscles in knots of agony.

It never came.

A high-pitched scream erupted from his right. Chris spun, his eyes snapping open to see Liz crumpling to the ground. The color fled her face as she clutched desperately at her throat. Her feet drummed against the soft floor and a strangled scream escaped her.

Then she fell silent, her last gasps of air stolen away.

Chris threw himself forward, desperate to reach her, but strong arms grasped him around the waist and hauled him back. He lashed out with his elbow, catching the guard in the face, and the hands released him. He glimpsed the man falling backwards, the other stepping towards him, but he was already at Liz's side, reaching out, grabbing her by the wrist…

A jolt of electricity flashed between them, and Chris was hurled across the room.

Coming to rest a few feet away, Chris shook his head and struggled to sit up. Liz still writhed against the soft floor, her back arching, her mouth wide and gasping. Her fingers clawed at her throat, tearing at the collar's metal chain. But there was no dislodging the steel links.

Halt stepped between them, a grim smile on his serpent lips. "Seventy-five milliamps," he said, shaking his head. "Enough to cause severe muscle contractions, respiratory failure, death."

Behind him, Liz was as pale as a ghost, her throws of agony already growing weaker. Her mouth opened, gasping like a fish out of water. Yet somehow, her crystal eyes found his. Shining with tears, they pierced him, conveying her silent command.

Don't give in!

A sob rattled up from Chris's chest as he closed his eyes, unable to watch any longer. Bowing his head, he cradled his shattered fist. Despair rose within him, overwhelming.

"*Please!*" His cry echoed from the one-way mirror.

A sudden stillness came over the room. Lying on the ground, Chris did not move, unable to look, to witness the consequence of his defiance. So long as he did not look, he could deny the truth.

Liz couldn't be gone, couldn't be dead.

But in his heart, Chris knew he had to face the truth. Blinking back tears, he sucked in a breath and lifted his head.

Liz lay where she had fallen, her limbs splayed out at random angles, the tangles of her hair caught on her face. The collar shone from her neck, the red light finally gone out.

Staring at her broken body, a pit opened in Chris, a gulf of despair that threatened to swallow him whole. A desperate sob tore from his throat, a cry of anguish, a plea for life. Lifting himself, he crawled towards her. He could feel his strength failing, the last drops of energy leaving him, but with a final lunge he reached out and grasped her wrist.

At his touch, Liz's chest moved. A soft cough came from the fallen girl as her eyelids fluttered.

"*What?*" Halt snarled.

The door clicked again, and Doctor Fallow stepped into the room.

27

"Enough, Halt," Angela said, so angry she was almost tripping over the words.

Halt turned to stare at her, eyes wide, his surprise already turning to rage. She knew she'd crossed a line by defying him now. This time, there were no other doctors to back her up—the others were still tending to the survivors of the PERV-B strain.

"Excuse me?" Halt sounded almost bemused.

"I said, that's enough," Angela repeated, mustering her courage.

A few moments ago, she had been driven to act. Watching Halt's cruelty, his determination to bend the candidates to his will at any cost, had pushed her over the edge. Whatever good she'd hoped might come from her work, it was not worth this. Halt's actions were brutal and pointless and wasteful, a display that did nothing more than serve the man's ego.

And Angela could not bear to watch the girl die. She could not shake that feeling of kinship, could not help but see her own youthful self in the girl's eyes.

So she had acted. She had superseded Halt's controller from within the observation room, disabling the collars of the two subjects. As supervisor of the project, her watch had precedence over every other controller in the building—even Halt's.

This isn't right. The words whispered in her mind as she looked at the boy and girl. *They're just kids.*

Biting her lip, she straightened, preparing herself for Halt's rage. "There's no justifying this, Halt. They passed the test. The project is a success. But this…" She waved a hand to indicate the girl. "This display is pointless. I won't allow it."

Halt shifted on his feet. A strange calm seemed to have come over him. "You won't allow it?"

Angela found herself retreating a step, though the doctor had not moved. "No," she said, shaking her head. "I've disabled their collars."

"You forget yourself, doctor." Halt still spoke in a soft voice. "These displays of insolence…are becoming problematic."

"They are *my* candidates, Halt."

For a moment, he did not reply. His eyes studied her, sweeping over her body, cold and calculating. Angela lifted her chin, facing him down.

At last, Halt nodded. He waved to the guards. "Get them up. Return them to their cell."

As the guards started toward Christopher and Elizabeth, Halt turned back to Fallow. He stood deathly still, poised in the center of the room as the guards shepherded the two teenagers from the testing room. His eyes did not blink, never left Angela's face. Only when the door clicked shut did he step towards her.

"Just because their parents were traitors—"

"*How dare you?*" Halt interrupted, almost shouting now.

Fallow found herself retreating from the man's rage, but in just two steps she found herself pressed up against the mirror, the cold glass at her back, with nowhere left to look but the doctor.

Halt came at her in a rush, his hand flashing out to catch her by the throat. His fingers clenched tight as she opened her mouth to scream, stealing away her voice. His lips drew back in a scowl as he leaned in.

With a sudden, violent shove, Halt slammed her head back into the glass. Stars spun across Angela's vision and her knees went weak. Pain lanced through her skull as Halt pulled her towards him, until their faces were less than an inch apart.

"If you *ever* defy me again, I will see you in a cage with your precious candidates," he ground out through clenched teeth.

Red exploded across Angela's vision as he slammed her into the mirror again. Then the fingers released her, and with a muffled sob she slumped to the ground.

Halt looked down at her, open contempt in his eyes. "The experiment will continue," he said. "I will see that the final doses are administered to the candidates. Those still unconscious will remain in their comas until our research has been completed."

Darkness swept across Angela's vision, rising up to claim her. She fought to hold it off as Halt crouched beside her.

"Tell me doctor, you aren't really so naïve, are you?" he asked, his voice taken on an amused tone. "Did you truly buy the company line?"

"What?" Fallow croaked, her mind swamped, unable to piece together the meaning behind Halt's words.

The man chuckled. "Their parents were never traitors, Fallow," he said.

"Then who?" Fallow whispered, her heart pounding in her ears.

Halt shrugged as he stood. "People who wouldn't be missed, or those who might have stood in our way at the wrong time." His grin spread. "Anyone we could find, really."

"No..."

"Yes," Halt cut her off, "and if you don't want to be the next on the executioner's block, I suggest you return to your laboratory. If our new virus succeeds, I might just let you live."

❧ 28 ❧

C *lang.*

Chris slumped to the ground as the cell door slid closed behind them. Liz staggered past him and toppled onto Ashley's bed. The guards had practically carried her this far. Despite faring slightly better than Chris in the fight, her collar had left its mark. The damage ran deep, each inhalation bringing an awful coughing and gurgling from her chest.

Unfortunately, Chris wasn't in much better shape.

Whatever Halt had said about success, Chris still lacked the relentless strength of the *Chead*. When it had caught him, no amount of skill, training or mutated muscle had been enough to save him from its grasp.

Thank God for Liz, he thought.

She lay sprawled across the bed, her face half-buried in the pillow, her back rising with each labored breath. Every few seconds she would groan, but otherwise she lay still.

Getting to his hands and knees, Chris crawled across the cell to Sam's bed and pulled himself up. Under the circumstances, he didn't think the others would mind if they borrowed them. Both beds were neatly made up, the covers pulled tight, the presence of their two friends wiped clean.

Minutes slipped by as he lay there, his face throbbing where the *Chead* had struck him. After a time, the clang of the outer door carried down the corridor. Idly, Chris wondered if someone had come to finish the job the *Chead* had started. There was no one else inside the prison block now. The other cells were empty, the faces that had once lined the corridor either dead or gone.

No, whoever it was had come for them.

Unable to summon the energy to move, Chris lifted an eyelid and looked out into the corridor. A woman stood outside the bars, her hands fiddling nervously with the hem of her lab coat. For a second he thought it was Fallow, before he realized she was too young, her hair blonde instead of brown. A guard stood beside the woman, looking bored.

"I'm...I'm to give you a round of antibiotics," she squeaked.

On the opposite bed, Liz did not so much as stir. Stifling a groan, Chris rolled onto his side. "Really?"

he coughed. "You people are all of a sudden concerned for our wellbeing?"

The woman gave a nervous nod. "Could you, could you get to the back of the cell, please?"

Chris blinked. If he hadn't been in so much pain, he would have laughed. Instead he looked at Liz, then back at the doctor. "Sorry, lady. But I don't think we're going anywhere."

"But…but you're meant to…"

Closing his eyes, Chris lay back on the bed. "Just get it over with. Have the guard ready to press his little button, if it makes you feel better."

The woman hesitated another second, and then nodded. A buzzer sounded and the cell door slid open. The little doctor hopped into the cell, a packet of syringes held in one hand, a vial of clear liquid in the other.

Briefly, Chris contemplated resisting. After everything they'd been through, he distrusted even this harmless-looking woman. Who knew what new horror might wait in the vial? But a hollow feeling sat in his stomach, an awful, helpless weakness that sapped him of the will to fight.

After all, what was the point in fighting now? It was too late—they'd already lost, had already been damaged beyond repair.

Chris slumped into his pillow and watched as the woman stopped beside Liz.

"She's unconscious," she said, sounding

surprised. "I thought…I thought the experiment was a success."

"You'll have to ask your boss about that." Chris paused, his thoughts drifting. "Where are our friends? What's happening to them?"

The woman was busy preparing her syringe, and it was a moment before she answered. It wasn't until she leaned over Liz that he heard her whisper. "The others are being kept in their comas," she breathed. "To make the change easier."

Chris watched as the woman inserted the needle into the middle of Liz's back and depressed the plunger. Then she moved over to him, the needle disappearing into a bag marked *Biological Waste*. Another appeared as she raised the vial.

Turning away, Chris winced as the needle pinched his back. The cold tingle of the injection spread between his shoulder blades as the woman stepped back. To his relief, there was no pain, and the cold sensation quickly faded.

"Are we done, Doctor Faulks?" came the guard's voice from outside the cell.

"Yes." Chris glanced up at the sound of retreating footsteps. He watched the woman reach the door and turn back, her eyes catching in his. "I'm sorry."

Then she was gone.

Chris frowned, already resigning himself to whatever fresh torment had been in the injection. He was certain now it had not been antibiotics. Something in the doctor's face as she looked back, in her final words, had warned him.

At least this time there was no pain.

A gurgling sound came from Liz's bed, drawing Chris's attention back to his friend. She had rolled onto her back now, her mouth wide and gasping. Her eyes were closed, her brow creased as though she were struggling to wake. Fingers clenched at the sheets and the veins stood up against her neck.

Chris's heart lurched and a sense of urgency gripped him. Careful to protect his injured hand, he rolled from the bed and crawled across to the other set of bunks. Pulling himself up beside Liz, he reached for her as she started to thrash. A wild arm swung out, catching him in the face, and her foot struck a pole, making the bunk shake. Another awful gurgle came from her chest.

"Liz, Liz, *stop*," Chris shouted, struggling to calm her.

With growing fear, he realized what was happening to her. She was choking, drowning in the fluid filling her lungs.

Ignoring the agony in his hand now, Chris caught Liz by the shoulder as another convulsion took her. He pulled her close, fighting to hold her, to turn her on her side. Desperate fists beat against him, and fire ripped up his arm as she struck his broken hand.

Gasping, he twisted, and narrowly avoided a wild thrust of her knee.

Chris heaved, pulling Liz onto her side. As she rolled, he saw her eyes were wide open and staring, though it was clear she remained unconscious. Bloodshot veins threaded the whites of her eyes, and a trickle of blood ran from her nose, staining the white of her pillow.

As she settled onto her side, a ragged gasp tore from her lips. Her chest rose, the gurgling fading to a whispered cough. She gulped again, wheezing in the cool air, as though still struggling to take in enough oxygen. Chris tilted her head forward slightly, memories of a high school first aid class guiding him.

Moving her upper arm, he placed the hand beneath her head, then pulled her knee up towards her chest. Liz's breathing eased as she settled into the Recover Position, the gurgling fading as her airways cleared.

Finally, Chris let out a long sigh, satisfied that for the moment she was safe. Holding her in place, he sent out a silent thanks that Liz was so small.

Only then did his own weariness return. His head sank onto the pillow as he watched Liz, a smile pulling at his lips. Her eyes had closed again, her lips parted just a fraction. A wisp of hair fluttered against her nose with each exhalation.

As the adrenaline faded, the sharp throb of

Chris's hand returned. He stifled a groan of his own, eager not to disturb Liz now that she had settled.

Closing his eyes, he saw her again in the padded room, thrashing on the floor, and felt again the awful helplessness. He shuddered and pushed the image away.

Only Fallow's intervention had saved her, saved them both.

Fallow.

The woman's face drifted through his mind. She had been a part of this from the start, had admitted her role in this whole project while helping them prepare for their fight.

You are the culmination of my life's work.

Was that why she had saved them, why she'd stopped Halt from killing Liz? Or was there more to it? Had the woman's conscience gotten to her?

Chris struggled to concentrate, but cobwebs tangled with his thoughts, and he could find no answers to his questions. His body throbbed, the ache of a dozen bruises dulling his mind. Heat radiated from Liz, banishing the cold of the cell. Distantly, he felt the pull of sleep.

His eyes fluttered open, catching a glimpse of Liz. The pained twist of her lips had faded, revealing a softness in her face, the kindness of the girl hidden within. Her breathing had quieted now, and her eyes quivered beneath her eyelids, lost in some dream.

The weight of exhaustion slowly dragged Chris's

eyes shut again. He knew he should move, should return to his own bed, but he could not find willpower. His last ounce of energy had fled.

Within seconds, the soft wrappings of sleep had claimed him.

❊ 29 ❊

Light burned at Liz's eyelids, dragging her from her dreams, back to the pain. It washed over her like rain, a tingle that burned in her every muscle. Gritting her teeth, she willed the agony to fade, to release her from its fiery grip. Slowly it slipped away, until only embers remained.

Liz took a breath, suppressing a groan as the ache returned, now an icy frost that filled her lungs. Then she paused as movement came from beside her. Cracking open an eye, she found Chris asleep beside her. She frowned, the beginnings of anger curling in her stomach. Then a dim memory surfaced, of water all around her, of drowning in a bottomless ocean, of fire in her chest as she breathed the salty liquid. Then...Chris's hands on her shoulders, pulling her up, dragging her to the surface. The relief of fresh air, filling her lungs, of oxygen flooding her body.

Her anger vanished, replaced by a warmth that swept away the pain. She looked at Chris, watching the soft rise and fall of his chest, the flickering of his eyelids. She remembered her fear as the *Chead* beat him to the ground, the terror that had risen within her. Yet instead of panic, it had filled her with purpose, with the need to act, to save him.

A moan came from Chris and he wriggled beneath the thin blanket, drawing closer. Slowly his eyes cracked open.

"You know, when I said I'd give you a chance, I didn't mean it as an invite…" she teased, a playful smile tugging at her lips.

She caught him as he flinched away. Gently taking up his good hand, she pulled him back, drawing him closer, until only an inch separated them.

"Don't," she murmured, basking in the heat of his body. "Don't."

His hazel eyes stared back at her, bloodshot but clear, and filled with…something. She leaned in, trying to make out what, and her mouth brushed against his. A jolt of energy passed between them, and then she was kissing him.

She felt Chris grow tense, and for a second thought he would pull away.

Then his hand was in her hair, and he was kissing her back, his lips hard against hers. A prickling came from her hip as he gripped her. Blood pounded in her ears, spreading outwards until her entire body was tingling. She wrapped her arms around Chris, holding him tight, leaving no escape. Goosebumps prickled her skin as fingers slid to the small of her back.

The scent of him filling her nostrils, Liz parted her lips, her tongue flicking out to taste him. His tongue found hers, and they danced to a rhythm all of their own. Her mind fell away, drowned by the rush of blood to her head. Her pain was forgotten, replaced by threads of pleasure winding through her body. Her skin was aflame, burning wherever he touched.

She slid her fingers through his hair, pulling him deeper into the kiss. Hunger filled her then, a need that grew with every heartbeat. A moan slipped from her lips and she gripped him hard, desperate now.

Chris flinched in her arms and she paused, remembering his broken hand. For a moment they slowed, but their lips did not part, their tongues still dancing, tasting. Liz wriggled in under his arm, her chest pounding like a drum as he held her.

Liz drew back then, sucking in a breath. Opening her eyes, she looked at him, saw the smile tugging at his lips. She shivered, a memory rising of the horror from the day before. A sour taste filled her mouth, the pain returning. She blinked, and a tear streaked her cheek.

"What are we doing, Chris?" she whispered.

Chris pulled back, his eyes sad. Reaching out, he wiped away her tear, then kissed her on the forehead. "What do you mean?"

"What's the point?" she choked, closing her eyes, the darkness welling within. "They could kill us tomorrow, mutate us beyond recognition, burn the last traces of humanity from us, like that thing—"

She broke off as Chris kissed her again, fast and hard. He pulled back, looking her in the eye. "We can't let them win, Liz," he whispered. "They've taken so much from us already, used us, stolen our humanity. But they can't take our spirit, our hope. It's all we have left. And I won't let them take it."

"Haven't they already?"

Chris only smiled. "Not yet. It's like Ashley said —they're only human. They'll make mistakes." The fingers of his good hand found hers, and squeezed. "When they do, we'll be ready."

Staring into his eyes, Liz could almost bring herself to believe.

Almost.

Still, he was right. They couldn't let their captors win. For the moment, they still had each other. She would not let them take that from her too. Leaning in, Liz gave herself to the fire burning within. Their mouths locked and she pressed herself hard against him, her hands sliding beneath his shirt. A wild hunger filled her, her kisses becoming ravenous. His arm went around her again, gripping her with a new fierceness. His lips left hers as he pulled away—then they were at her neck, stoking the flames within.

She groaned, arching backwards, her fingers tight in his hair.

His hands slid beneath her shirt, trailing down her back, tingling wherever they touched. The warmth inside her spread, and she started to tremble. Lost in her passion, she leaned in and nipped at his neck.

Liz smiled as Chris gave a little yelp. His hands continued to roam, though they had not yet gone far enough for her liking. She slid her fingers through the buttons of his shirt and began to undo them. A fine layer of hair covered his chest, which was surprising muscular. His skin was hot beneath her fingers.

She groaned as Chris's mouth found its way to the small of her throat. With a rush of impatience she helped him with her own buttons, knowing his good hand was already occupied. His lips slid lower, his tongue darting out, tasting her, even as his hand etched invisible trails across the soft skin of her back.

Then he paused, his fingers stilling on her back. Liz stifled a moan as she opened her eyes. She found him staring up at her from between the folds of her breasts, fear sparkling in his eyes. Her stomach twisted as ice slid down her spine.

"What?" she whispered.

"There's…there's something wrong. There are… lumps," Chris replied softly.

Liz's cheeks burned, but her fear fell away. Laughing softly, she shook her head. Her hands slid through his hair, drawing him to her, until his lips brushed across her nipples. She arched her back as Chris groaned. Barely able to catch her breath, Liz slid her hands lower, sliding them beneath his waistband, reaching for him…

But he pulled away again, shaking his head. "No," he said, his cheeks reddening, "not…not those."

The hackles rose on Liz's neck at the look on his face. Her lust went from her in a rush. "What?"

"On your back," Chris said, barely breathing. "There's…something on your back."

Again, fear flooded Liz. Sitting upright, she craned her neck, straining to see. Her movements grew frantic as she fumbled at her shirt, tugging at the collar, desperate to rid herself of it. Chris reached out, trying to calm her, but she pushed him away. Fabric tore and the shirt came loose. Throwing it aside, she twisted her neck again and looked.

Beside her, Chris's face was flushed, a flicker of desire still lurking in his eyes. But in that moment she no longer cared. Her naked back shone in the fluorescent lights, the lumps unmistakable. They bulged in the center of her back, on either side of her spine, midway between her arms and hips.

Pressure grew in Liz's chest, escaping as a low whine, a muffled scream. Horror swept through her, a raging anger at the doctors, at their violation of her body. Another shriek built, but she swallowed it down, blinking back tears.

Her eyes burned as she looked at Chris, saw the fresh tears in his eyes.

"Where does it stop?" she whispered.

🐝 30 🐝

Within hours, Chris discovered the same growths on his own back. Though there was no pain or discomfort, they ignited a terror that threatened to overwhelm him. Whatever the doctors had done to them, it seemed they'd failed after all.

They made a mistake. The words whispered in his thoughts, along with something else, a familiar word, a horror from his childhood.

Cancer.

The memory of his father's illness still lay heavy on his mind—the wasting sickness, the slow loss of strength, of life. Despite its ferocity, his father had fought back, had even won, for a time. But cancer was like a weed, always there, waiting to return. It wore you down, drew the life from you one drop at a time.

And his father, once larger than life, had been laid low.

As the hours ticked past, Chris could think of no other explanation for the lumps. Vicious and unrelenting, the cancers would spread through their bodies, poisoning their blood, feeding on their strength, until there was nothing left but empty husks.

Lying on the bed, he held Liz in his arms, each alone in their own thoughts.

The next day, they woke to the first beginnings of pain. It began as a soft twitch in the center of his back, radiating outwards from the strange protrusions. The ache pulsed, flickering with the beat of his heart, but growing sharper with each intake of breath. Hour by hour it spread, threaded its way into his chest, until it hurt just to breathe.

For Liz, it was worse. When she woke she could barely speak. Her skin had lost its color; even the angry red marks beneath her collar had paled to white. By lunch she could no longer lie on her back, and when he touched her forehead, he found her skin burning with fever.

Each hour the lumps grew. Their skin stretched and hardened around the protrusions, darkening to purple bruises. Each bulge was unyielding to their scrutinizing prods, and soon tiny black spots appeared on their surfaces.

When the lights woke them on the third day,

Chris could hardly move from the pain. Agony wove its way through his torso, spreading out like the roots of a tree, engulfing his lungs, reducing each breath to a battle, a desperate fight for life.

The next time a guard arrived with food, Chris could no longer tell whether it was breakfast or dinner. He blinked hard into the light, pain lancing his skull. The room spun and then settled into a double image. His stomach churned as two Liz's appeared to stand over him, offering a bowl of dark-colored stew. He saw her waver on her feet, and blindly took the bowl before she fell.

Sitting back, he raised a shaking spoonful of broth to his mouth, but there was no taste when he swallowed. His stomach swirled again, then he began to heave. He barely made it to the toilet. A moment later, Liz was beside him at the sink.

Afterwards, Chris slid to the ground, his head throbbing in the blinding light. Liz sat with him, her head settling on his shoulder. For a moment the pain faded, giving in to a wave of warmth. He closed his eyes, savoring Liz's closeness, but the relief did not last long. His stomach lurched again, and he released Liz and crawled back to the toilet.

The *clang* of the lights going out was a welcome relief.

Stomach clenched, lungs burning, head thumping, Chris returned to the beds. Stars danced across his vision, but he hauled himself up, no longer caring whose bed it was. The room stank of vomit and spilled food, of unwashed bodies and blood. The scent of chlorine had long since been overwhelmed.

Caught in the clutches of fever, Chris lost all track of time. At some point he felt Liz's body beside him. He drew comfort from the heat of her presence, in the closeness of her face. Then her face warped, and it felt as though his own body was distorting, and he forced his eyes closed.

Wild colors spun through his mind as time passed. At one point he remembered calling out, begging the guards to come, to bring the doctors, to bring anyone. But no one came, no one responded, and he soon gave up asking for help. He started asking for death instead.

In his dreams, he saw his body slowly decaying, watched his veins turn black, his arms begin to rot. Then he would find himself whole, riding in the passenger seat of his father's '68 Camaro, his dad driving, an infectious grin on his youthful face. A moment later he was in a hospital, the smell of bleach and the beeping of machinery all around. And his father, lying in a bed, his arms withered, his face lined with age. Only the smile was unchanged.

The image faded, and Chris was back in the cell, back with the pain. Looking at his arms, he wondered what was real, what was not. One instant it was night, the next the blinding light of day, then back to black. At times he would wake, gasping for air, shivering beneath the blanket, and know in his heart he was dying.

Once, he dreamed that he was flying, soaring through mountains, far from the nightmares of their prison cell.

Then he woke.

It was a long time before Chris realized he was no longer dreaming. He shivered as the cold air wrapped around him, but otherwise there was no discomfort. The pain had vanished, and for a second he considered the possibility that he was dead. Then a groan came from someone nearby, and he knew he was not alone.

Forcing open his eyes, he peered out from the shadow of his bunk bed, searching for Liz.

The first thing he realized was that they hadn't been alone in their fever dreams. Someone had entered the cell while they slept, and cleaned the vomit and blood from the room. Liz lay in the opposite bed, covered by a strange-looking blanket of black feathers. She shifted beneath it, then blinked across at him, raising a hand to shield her face. Her lips parted as she licked her cracked lips.

"Chris?" she croaked.

"I'm here," he replied, his throat raw. A desperate thirst clutched him, and he looked to the sink, wondering if he had the strength to reach it.

In the other bed, Liz slowly sat up, the blanket still clinging to her. Dimly, Chris made to do the same, but a weight on his back pressed him down. Reaching back, he felt soft feathers brush his hand. He shrugged, trying to dislodge the blanket as he lifted himself to his hands and knees.

Chris paused, a distant thought tugging at his memories, but it faded again before he could catch it. He cast a questioning look at Liz, but she said nothing. He clenched his fists, feeling a wrongness about himself, but unable to trace the source.

Shaking his head, Chris pushed the last of the fever dreams away and rolled out of the bed onto his feet. To his surprise, the weight came with him, pushing him forward. Off-balance, he crashed to the floor in a tangle of limbs and feathers.

"Chris?" Liz's voice shook.

Confused, Chris frowned at her from the floor. He pulled himself up, but the weight still clung to his back. Only sheer determination kept him from toppling over backwards. He froze when he saw the look on Liz's face.

Eyes wide, she sat half-crouched on the bed. Her mouth opened and closed, but no sound came out. Her arm shook as she raised it and pointed. Shivering, Chris looked behind him, fear of the unknown rippling down his spine. But his bed was empty, the feather blanket trailing out behind him.

Chris started to turn back to Liz, then paused. He blinked, staring at the tawny brown feathers of his blanket. There was something wrong about the way they hung between himself and the bed, something not quite right.

Stretching out a hand, Chris tried to dislodge the blanket from his shoulders. He flinched as his hand brushed against something unexpected, something hard beneath the blanket. Withdrawing his hand, he looked at Liz, but she still sat in silence, her mouth agape.

With a rush of courage, Chris reached behind his neck and ran a hand down his spine.

He found the growths where they had been before, midway down his back. They had changed—becoming long shafts that stretched far beyond his reach. A soft down of feathers covered their length, sprouting from his flesh as though they had every right to be there.

Wings.

His mind spun. He shook his head, refusing to face the truth, though they lay stretched out before his eyes. He trembled, and watched the shiver run down the wings, the tawny brown feathers quivering in the cool air.

A muffled sob came from the other bed. Liz had

struggled to her feet, revealing the long black wings hanging from her own back. They stretched out to either side of her, each at least ten feet long, the large black feathers tangling with the sheets on the bed. Where the feathers bent, Chris glimpsed soft white down beneath, small feathers curled in upon themselves, clinging close to her flesh. They shone in the overhead lights, seeming almost aflame, as though Liz was some avenging angel descended from heaven.

Wings.

Warmth spread through Chris's chest, mingling with the horror. A profound confusion gripped him: a disgust at this fresh violation, the further loss of his humanity—but also wonder, an awe for the trembling new limbs on his back.

Wings.

He looked at Liz. Her eyes were wide, glistening with tears. Her lips trembled, a shudder running through her body. Through her wings.

For the first time, Chris realized they were both naked. Strangely, it no longer seemed to matter. After all they had suffered, all that had been done to them, Chris's body hardly felt like his own. He felt apart from it now, separated from his nakedness.

A tear spilled down Liz's cheek, and he knew the same thought had occurred to her. He stepped across the room, struggling for balance, and pulled her to him. He shivered as her arms went around his waist and her head lifted, drawing him in.

A fire ignited in Chris's chest as their lips met. His hands slid up into her hair as her tongue darted out, sliding between his lips. The taste of her filled him, the intoxicating scent of her hair toying with his nostrils.

After a long minute, Liz pulled back. Raising a hand to her face, she wiped away her tears. She looked at her wings then, her lips twisting as though in thought. They hung limply from her back, feathers quivering, and he knew what she was thinking.

Liz closed her eyes, her face tightening, the lines of her jaw deepening. Her brow creased, and behind her the black-feathered wings twitched. They began to shake, then lifted slightly and half-opened. There they paused, as though lacking the strength to go any further.

Eyes still closed, Liz bit her lip, and persisted.

Bit by bit, her wings spread, until they seemed to fill the cell. They stretched more than twenty feet, twice the length of their beds, so that their tips poked out through the bars into the corridor.

Twenty feet of jet-black feathers, of curly white down, of a majestic, undefinable magic.

When Liz opened her eyes again, Chris saw the wonder there, the fear falling away before it.

At a nod from her, he shut his own eyes and sought to do the same. Reaching down into the depths of his consciousness, he followed the tingle that came from his back, the newfound sensations originating from the limbs. As he concentrated, the tingle spread along his spine. The hairs stood up on his neck as new connections formed within his mind. His neurons flared into life, recognizing the presence of new muscles and bone and flesh.

A tremor shook the weight on his back. There was a wrongness to that weight, an awkward presence to it, like clothes that did not quite fit. But opening his mind, he tried to accept it, to embrace it.

At last, Chris opened his eyes. A sharp *crack* sounded as his wings snapped open, unfurling to fill the room. Feathers as long as his forearm brushed against the far wall, touched the bars of the cell, and he *felt it*, sensed the pressure against his feathers.

He grinned at Liz, unable to keep the wonder from his face. She grinned, laughed, opened her arms to embrace him.

With a deafening shriek, an alarm began to sound.

🙚 32 🙙

Angela strode around the corner and started towards the wide iron door at the end of the corridor. Heavy locking bars stretched across the dull metal, and a guard stood to either side, watching her approach. Each held a heavy rifle and wore the familiar trigger watch on his wrist. With a flick of a finger, the watches could activate all collars in their immediate vicinity, incapacitating any threat the prisoners within might pose.

Or at least, that was the idea.

Today, the watches had been reduced to worthless pieces of steel and glass. Just minutes before, Angela had entered her code to deactivate all the collars inside the facility. Halt, in his arrogance, had thought her cowed by his violence, that her fear would prevent her fighting back after his proclamation.

Instead, his revolution had given Angela the resolve to act.

Left alone in the padded room, fading in and out of consciousness, Angela had finally seen the true futility of her research. It had never been about a cure, or a weapon to fight the *Chead*. It had always been about *this*, this need for power, for a weapon to use against their enemies.

Whatever the cost.

And Angela knew, threats or no, she could not allow the project to continue.

Climbing to her feet, the weight of regret heavy on her shoulders, Angela had settled on a new path.

Now the time to act had come, and she could not hesitate.

Ahead, the guards pulled back the bolts, and the iron door swung open with a *screech*. Angela walked past the guards without breaking stride, nodding as she went.

A hushed silence hung over the narrow corridor within, as faces turned towards her. Another *screech* and the door swung shut, sealing her inside. Sucking in a shuddering breath, Angela started forward, careful to keep to the center of the hall, beyond the reach of grasping arms.

Stone-grey eyes followed her down the passage.

Tension hung like a blanket on the air as she made her way past the cells. Hate radiated from the dark creatures pressing up against the prison bars.

There were meant to be ten in all: five boys, five girls.

Ten vicious killing machines, hungry for blood, for freedom.

The *Chead* watched her as she reached the corridor's end and turned back. There she paused, a frown crossing her face as she looked into one of the cells. It was empty, one of the girls was missing.

It made no sense, but there was no time to adjust her plan. She had to act. Each of the creatures had been captured in the wilderness, or suffered the change in other experiments. Each was destined to die here, never again to feel the heat of the sun on their skin. Their eyes would never see the beauty of the mountains beyond the walls, their ears would never hear the roar of ocean waves.

Or at least, that had been Halt's intention.

The *Chead* wore the familiar steel collars on their neck, but because of Angela's interference, those collars were now little more than decorative necklaces.

Standing at the end of the corridor, Angela faced the exit. Cells stretched out on either side of her, the males to her left, females to her right. Something about the *change* accelerated the development and reproductive drive of the *Chead*. Left to their own devices, they bred like rabbits. And while most of the occupants appeared almost fully mature, the oldest was just thirteen years old.

Angela steeled herself and started back towards the exit. The grey eyes followed her, alive with intelligence, searching for an opportunity. One second, one slip; that was all they needed. Several men had already lost their lives by wandering too close to the bars. Angela would not make that mistake.

But she needed them to see her, to be awake.

To be ready.

As she approached the entrance to the prison block, the guard by the door reached out to open it. She glanced at his face as she passed, a flicker of guilt touching her. But it was too late for regrets now. It was time.

As the door reached its apex, Angela looked at her watch. It was more advanced than the others, controlling more than just the candidate's collars. As head geneticist and supervisor of the project, she had control over many of the security protocols in the facility. Halt had not thought it necessary to override them.

Angela pressed her finger to the touchscreen.

Behind her, a buzzer screeched, followed by the rattling of cell doors opening. Angela leapt forward as the guards looked up, confusion turning quickly to open terror as the *Chead* emerged from their cages. The men stood frozen as Angela darted past them and began to run.

The screams of the dying chased her down the corridor.

———

Angela's breath came in ragged gasps as she took a corner. From behind her came the roar of gunfire and the howls of the *Chead*. Overhead, lights flashed, and somewhere in the building a siren screeched. Muffled voices erupted from speakers along the corridors, a robotic voice asking her not to panic.

The thump of approaching boots came from ahead. She tensed as two guards raced into view, then relaxed as they sprinted past her, guns held at the ready. Their eyes barely registered her, but she saw their fear. Just as well. With a nine *Chead* loose in the building, they would be hard-pressed to survive.

A minute later she drew up outside the other prison block. She had hesitated before detouring here —only two of the seven survivors from the PERV-A strain were locked within. But Elizabeth was here, with her haunting blue eyes, and Angela could not bring herself to abandon the girl.

Fortunately, the guards had already abandoned their posts—though whether to face the *Chead* or run, she wasn't sure. The door to the cell block had been left open, and she stepped inside, shivering as her eyes swept over the rows of empty cells.

So much loss.

Angela closed her eyes, regret welling within her. How had she been so blind? She had allowed her ambition to surpass caution, to blind her to the atrocities within the facility. Her morals, her integrity, all had been lost because of her drive to succeed.

And these children had paid the price.

Moving down the corridor, Angela searched for the two she had come for. She froze when she found them, her breath catching in her throat.

She had seen them in their fever-induced sleep, had seen the others in their comas. She already knew the experiment had succeeded; that the homeotic genes had taken. Stimulated by the final injection, they acted like a master switch, triggering the cluster of genes embedded in the candidates' genomes. The genes corresponding to wing growth.

Angela had watched the wings grow, watched the feathers sprout like seedlings from their skin. Even so, she was not prepared for the sight that greeted her.

Elizabeth and Christopher stood in all their glory, wings spread wide, stretching out to fill the cell. They had found the ragged clothes she'd left by their beds, with the clumsy holes she'd torn in the backs. The girl's black feathers pressed against the brown of the boy's, their wings entwining in the tiny space.

Angela's heart ached with the wonder of it.

"What's happening?" Christopher demanded.

Blinking, Angela tore herself from her stupor. She shook her head, then looked down at her watch and pressed a button. The cell door slid open with a dull rattle.

The two of them stood within, looks of wary surprise appearing on their faces.

"Come on," Angela said. "We're getting out of here. Hurry, the others should be awake by now."

Christopher's hand drifted to his collar. Angela shook her head and reached into her pocket. "They're deactivated." Finding the little key, she tossed it to the girl. "Here, that'll unlock them. But *hurry*."

Within seconds, their collars lay discarded on the ground. Angela watched them embrace, saw the tears shining in their eyes, but she could not pause to celebrate their freedom. Apprehension nibbled at her stomach, an awful fear that they would be caught.

"*Come on*," she urged again, waving them towards the door. "We need to find the others."

Their eyes widened then, their mouths opening in question, but she was already moving away. Sirens still sounded and red lights flashed in the ceiling, but there was no sign of movement as they re-entered the corridors. The guards remained preoccupied at the other end of the facility, and she hoped the other civilians would have already retreated to the safe room by now.

Silently, she led them through the maze of the facility, to the isolation room where the other survivors of the PERV-A strain had remained in their drug induced comas. She had swapped out their medication that morning, replacing them with saline.

They would be awake by now, and she prayed they had not wandered from the room while she detoured.

Unfortunately, the surviving PERV-B candidates were lost to her. They still lay in their comas, their bodies wracked with fever, struggling to accept the chromosomal alterations of the virus. There was nothing she could do for them now.

Ahead, the door to the isolation room lay unguarded. She smiled, glad her distraction had proven so effective. With luck, they'd be long gone before anyone noticed their absence. If the guards even managed to regain control of the facility. She had seen a single *Chead* tear a man to pieces. With nine...she didn't like to think what nine *Chead* might be capable of.

But there was no more time to think of that. Angela pushed open the door and led the way inside.

IV

ESCAPE

❧ 33 ❧

Liz stumbled through the door after Chris. Every step was a struggle to keep upright. The new weight on her back threw her whole coordination out of sync, leaving her feeling strangely out of proportion. Even the simple act of closing her wings had taken several attempts, but she and Chris had finally managed to pull them tight against their backs. Even so, they niggled at her consciousness, an alien presence that would not go away.

The thought of freedom drove her on, and the knowledge that each step carried her closer to a possible reunion with Ashley and Sam. She sucked in a breath, savoring the feel of her naked neck. The collar was gone, her throat free of its steel encasing. It felt like a lifetime ago since she'd put on the awful contraption. Perhaps it was.

Blinking, Liz returned her mind to the present.

Looking around, she recognized the room they had awoken in after their first injection. Beds still lined its length, but they were empty now. The whir of machines filled the air, their tubes and wires dangling free. Her chest contracted as her eyes swept the room, searching for her friends.

A thud came from their right, and she spun, raising her fists to defend herself.

Then she lowered them. Beside her, Chris chuckled. Together they watched the figure sprawled on the ground struggling to sit up.

It took a few seconds for Sam to get his tangle of arms, legs and copper wings under control, and several more before he managed to stand. A string of curses echoed from the walls as he finally pulled himself up, red in the face, puffing like he'd run a marathon. Then Liz's eyes drifted past Sam, and she gave a wild yelp.

Ashley strode forward, her lips twitching with suppressed humor. She moved with the same casual grace as before, her long legs easily finding their balance as she weaved between the empty beds. Trailing out behind her, a pair of snow-white wings shone in the overhead lights. They quivered as she moved, slowly lifting from the ground, expanding across the room.

Liz laughed again as the two of them came together in a hug. She clung to her friend for a moment, Ashley's grip just as tight. When they finally broke apart, Ashley looked past Liz and raised an eyebrow at the doctor.

When Fallow did not speak, Ashley nodded and turned back to Liz. "I guess we found their weakness."

Chris shrugged. "She found us."

The distant wail of sirens prickled at Liz's ears, reminding her they weren't out of danger yet. Before she could speak, though, another movement came from the far side of the room. Beyond Sam, she found the remaining survivors of the project.

Her heart sank as she looked at Richard and Jasmine. Their attitude towards the four of them didn't seem to have changed in the untold weeks they'd lain unconscious. They stood on the far side of the room, arms crossed and eyes hard with suspicion. But it was not their faces that drew her attention. Their wings lay half-furled behind them, each sporting dark emerald feathers, like those of some tropical parrot. Their eyes caught hers and Liz quickly looked away, unable to face their unspoken accusations, their anger that she was alive, while Joshua was gone.

Of course, she thought. *Of everyone else who could have survived, it would be Richard and Jasmine…*

Well, Richard and Jasmine, and the girl.

Standing beside them was a young girl of maybe thirteen years. Locks of grey hair tumbled around her face, and her eyes were wide with fear. A button nose and freckled cheeks only served to make her look younger. How she could have survived this far, Liz could not begin to guess. She shivered as the girl's eyes, one blue, the other green, found her from across the room.

Looking away, Liz cast her gaze around the room one last time, searching for the others. There had still been dozens of candidates left the last time she had been there. But now there was only the seven of them, each sporting the plain grey uniforms they'd found at the ends of their beds.

"Where are the others?" she whispered, turning to face Fallow.

The doctor bowed her head. When she did not respond, Chris repeated Liz's question. "Doctor Fallow, where are the rest of them?"

Fallow looked back up, her eyes flashing. "Don't call me that. I don't deserve to be called 'doctor' after what I've done. My name is Angela." Her voice shook. "And the others did not survive. The physiological changes...their bodies could not support them. Even unconscious, the accelerated wing growth was too much. Their hearts gave out from the strain."

An awful anger spread through Liz as she stepped in close to the doctor. Fallow flinched, but this time she did not look away. "How many did you kill?" Liz hissed.

Angela Fallow closed her eyes. "I've lost count."

Her eyes snapped back open. "But it ends here. I won't let them take you too."

Liz might have struck her if Chris hadn't placed a hand on her shoulder. Looking at him, she saw the sadness in his eyes, the same sorrow from which her own rage spawned. She stepped away from Angela and hugged Chris to her. She smiled as Ashley joined them, then Sam.

"Ahem." Liz looked up at a new voice. Richard raised an eyebrow and tapped a finger to his collar. "Someone care to share the key?"

Chris nodded. Reaching into his pocket he pulled out the little key Angela had given them and handed it over. The clink of the thick steel collars striking the concrete followed as the five of them freed themselves.

"Are you okay there, Sam?" Chris asked, as Sam finally managed to unlock the clasp of his collar.

Sam cursed beneath his breath and tossed the collar aside. "Almost," he said, a shiver running through his copper feathers. Slowly his wings contracted. "Don't know what the idiots were thinking, putting these clunky things on our backs." He paused, eyeing Angela uncertainly. "Err, no offense, Doc—I mean, Angela?"

Angela shook her head, a sad smile touching her lips. "It's alright. You have every right to complain. I would have…I would have stopped them before they gave you the injection, but I was unconscious. Then I had to wait…until you were stable again."

"It's okay." Of all of them, Ashley seemed the best adapted to her new appendages. She looked over her shoulder, smiling. "I kind of like them."

"Yeah." Sam's voice was gruff, but he continued with his usual humor. "But yours are tiny. Did you have to make mine so *big?*"

Angela raised a hand to her mouth, trying to hide her smile. "It took some research of various avian species to get our specifications right. We looked at genome variation between Andean Condors and the Wandering Albatross to identify the genes relating to wing size in fragmented DNA from *Argentavis magnificens.*"

"Argentavis what?" Richard growled from nearby.

"The largest known bird to have flown," Jasmine said, surprising Liz.

Angela nodded. "It could weigh up to two-hundred fifty pounds. Once we'd identified all the genes related to wing surface area, we linked them with those controlling your own height and weight. Thus, why yours are so…big, Samuel."

Sam glanced at Ashley. "I think she's calling me fat…"

Smiling, Liz looked around their little group, a strange elation rising within her. Even with the open animosity of Jasmine and Richard, there was a connection between the seven of them now, a shared experience which could not be denied. Of all the desperate souls who had passed through this place, they alone had survived.

They alone had evolved.

"But why?" she asked suddenly, swinging on the doctor. "Why do any of this?"

"To stop the *Chead*," Angela whispered, "or at least, that's what we were told. The creatures are spreading, and humanity is hopelessly outmatched. We needed something more, soldiers able to match them for speed and power, who could detect their presence, whether in a crowd or a field of corn. Your strength, your senses, your wings, they were all meant for the sole purpose of hunting down the *Chead*."

"Were?" Ashley asked.

Angela shook her head. "I am afraid Halt and his superiors have ulterior motives."

"Not if I can help it," Sam growled and started towards the exit. "I don't know about you lot, but I'm about ready to leave."

"Wait!" Chris called him back. He looked at Angela. "What about our parents?"

"They're…not here," Angela replied shortly. "I'm sorry, Christopher, but we can do nothing for them here. Your friend is right, it's time we left."

There was a strange pitch to Angela's voice, and Liz sensed there was more she wasn't telling them. But before she could question the doctor further,

Angela started towards the door. The others exchanged glances, still processing the barrage of information. Feathers rustled as wings were furled, and then Chris started after her, Liz close behind.

Ahead of them, Angela was reaching out to open the door, when it suddenly swung inwards to meet her.

And Halt stepped into the room.

❧ 34 ❧

Liz froze at the sight of Halt, her heart dropping into the pit of her stomach. His eyes swept the room, widening, his brow wrinkling with rage. Before any of them could react, his gaze settled on Angela. Clutching a pistol in one hand, he sprang.

Angela managed a scream before he was on her, his arm wrapping around her waist, spinning her against him. Pressing the gun to her head, he drew back his lips.

"What do we have here, doctor?" Halt snarled. Angela flinched as he jabbed the gun into her ribs. "Have you betrayed me? Have you betrayed us all?"

Clenching her fists, Liz inhaled, scenting gunpowder in the air. Halt's gun had already been fired recently; this was no idle threat. A cold grin twisted his lips as Angela struggled in his grasp.

"*That's enough!*" he growled.

Halt swung the gun, catching Angela in the forehead. She slumped in his arms and he turned his attention on Liz and the others. "Don't come any closer."

Liz suppressed a moan. Angela had gone limp, but her eyes were still wide and staring. Her hands swiped feebly at Halt, but he was twice her size. Biting her lip, Liz glanced at the others. Her arms shook, the sensation spreading through her body, down her spine, to the foreignness of her wings. A phantom ache started in her throat, a distant reminder of the collar pressing against her flesh.

I won't go back.

She flinched as her fingernails dug into her palms. Drawing in a deep breath, she unclenched her hands, trying to calm herself, to find a way out of the trap. Her eyes travelled across the space between herself and Halt.

Too far.

But Chris was closer. From the corner of her eyes, Liz saw him slide another step towards the doctors. If he could reach Angela…

No, they were still too far away.

She looked back at Angela, seeing the emotion washing over the doctor's face—fear, anger, regret. The woman's head sagged as her eyes slid closed, her whole body trembling. Then her head snapped up, a new resolve now shining from her face. The fear had vanished, replaced by…

Liz opened her mouth to shout, but she was already too late. She wasn't sure what she would have said anyway. Would she have begged Angela not to act? Or had she only wanted to thank her, for finally freeing them?

Either way, Liz never got the chance. Angela jerked in Halt's arms, hurling her weight backwards. Small as she was, it was still enough to throw Halt off-balance. He cursed, struggling to recover.

In that instant, Chris charged. His wings snapped out to beat the air as he leapt, closing the gap in seconds. Arms wide, he reached for the doctor…

Boom.

The roar of the gun was so sudden, so deafening in the sealed room, that Liz found herself stumbling back in shock.

Then Chris barreled into Halt, his fist catching the man in the face, hurtling him through the air. He struck the floor with a dull thud, bounced once, before the concrete wall brought him to an abrupt stop. A low groan whispered from his lips as he slumped down and lay still. The gun slid across the floor, coming to rest in a nook between the floor and the wall.

Chris landed lightly on his feet, wings still outstretched, eyes locked on their tormentor. But Liz was already sprinting forward, falling to her knees beside Angela. A dark pool was spreading around the woman, the overhead lights glimmering on its scarlet surface. Her eyes were open, staring at the ceiling, her mouth wide in a silent scream. One hand still clutched at her chest, where a small red mark stained her lab coat.

Liz knelt beside her, tears misting her vision. A low moan came from her throat as she reached out and shook the woman. The soft pad of footsteps came from behind her, but she took no notice.

Disbelief threaded through her mind. Whatever her crimes, Angela Fallow had been the only one in this place to show the prisoners any compassion. Twice she had stopped Halt's torture, and in the end, she had followed her conscience, had freed them from their cells.

Now she was dead.

A terrible rage rose in Liz's chest, driving her to her feet. She leapt at Halt, crossing the room in a single bound. She reached down and grasped him by his lab coat, hauling him to his feet. Almost without effort she lifted him up and slammed him into the wall. He groaned, his eyelids flickering as she pinned him there, but he did not wake. Gritting her teeth, Liz drew back a fist.

Ashley caught her arm before the blow could fall. Liz half-turned, straining against the other girl, a snarl rumbling up from her chest. Frustration built inside her and she spun. Dropping Halt, she swung at Ashley instead.

Ashley leaned back and Liz's blow found only

open air. Her other hand shot out, catching Liz in the chest, pushing her back. Stumbling, Liz straightened and leapt at her. A terrible rage burned within her, filling Liz with a need to rend, to tear the flesh from her enemies.

"*Liz!*" Ashley yelled, raising an arm to protect herself.

The scream gave Liz pause. Blood pounding in her head, she drew back, even as a voice in her head shouted for her to attack. She sucked in a breath and the red haze faded, revealing the fear dancing in the eyes of her friends. Taking in another mouthful of air, she faced Ashley.

"*Why?*" she asked, her voice breaking. "Why did you stop me?"

"He's not worth it," Ashley breathed. "He's not, Liz. Don't let this place turn you into them. Don't let it make you a cold-blooded killer."

Liz clenched her fists, trembling with the effort to suppress her rage. Red light flickered across her vision as she looked down at Halt, and she fought the impulse to snap his neck.

She bowed her head. "He'll come for us," she whispered.

"They'll come for us anyway," Chris replied, placing a hand on her shoulder. "Besides, I doubt he'll be...*anything* after this. They were always talking about needing results." He waved a hand. "And this seems just about the opposite of that."

Slowly, Liz allowed her body to relax. Looking at Chris, she nodded.

He stepped forward then, arms opening, drawing her to him. They stood there in silence, holding each other, the others forgotten, the nightmare around them a distant memory.

When they finally parted, they turned to face the others. Ashley and Sam, Richard and Jasmine, and the strange little girl stared back. Their eyes shone with emotion: hope mixed with anger, love with hate. Shivering, Liz looked at Chris.

"Let's go."

35

The tired hinges of the door screeched as Chris threw himself against it. His shoulder throbbed, and his wings gave a little flap, but on the next blow the door caved. He stumbled after it, his momentum carrying him outside, where a blast of icy air caught in his wings and hurled him backwards. Pain shot through his bare feet as he stumbled on stones. Dropping to his knees, he braced himself against the howling wind, and glanced back at the others.

They filed out after him, one by one, their eyes alight with wonder. Turning, Chris looked out over a world blanketed in white. Flakes of snow swirled around them, drifting ever downwards, their intricate patterns catching in the light shining overhead. Clouds covered the sky, but after so long inside, it still seemed impossibly bright. Blinking back tears, Chris drank in the world around him.

Rocky mountains stretched high above them, sprouting like enormous trees from the slope on which they stood. Sheer escarpments of rock raced upwards, disappearing into the clouds, their surfaces white with ice. Farther down the valley the snow and ice gave way to barren rock.

Around the facility there were no trees or vegetation, only jagged gravel that promised to make walking difficult. They hadn't stopped to search for better equipment, and now Chris shivered as the icy air tore through his thin clothing. A dull ache began at the base of his skull, though despite their now undoubted height above sea level, his breath came easily.

Chris stared up the valley, his eyes trailing over the snow-covered boulders, up to where the slope disappeared into a narrow gorge. Glancing back down, he studied the valley as it fell away from the facility. There was not a sliver of cover in sight. Even so, down was tempting. Down would bring them to warmer air, out of the mountains, towards civilization. Perhaps they could find someone there to help them, to protect them from the monsters that would hunt them.

Steeling himself, Chris dismissed the temptation. It was the route their jailers would expect them to take, and without cover, the chase would be over before it began.

No, they needed to do the unexpected. They needed to go higher.

The others gathered, huddling close, wings wrapped tightly around their bodies to fend off the frigid air. His body trembling violently, Chris did the same, his wings curving around to encase him. The relief was instant, and the cold creeping through his chest vanished.

The others were watching him, wonder and fear mingling on their faces. They knew the next few hours would decide whether they lived or died. Whatever Angela had done to distract the guards, it wouldn't keep them busy forever. Before long, men with guns would come for them. Chris wanted to be far away by then.

Quickly he explained his plan, watching as Liz, Sam and Ashley nodded. Richard and Jasmine only stood in sullen silence, their faces expressionless, while the young girl hovered on the edge of the circle. So far they hadn't gotten a word from her. She huddled in close to Jasmine, a nameless, unknown quantity. Not for the first time, Chris wondered how she had survived Halt's trials.

When Chris finished speaking, he eyed Jasmine and Richard, expecting them to argue, but they only nodded. "Let's go then," Richard said abruptly.

Relieved, Chris turned and began the long trek

up towards the canyon. He moved as fast as the jagged gravel allowed him, wincing with each step. Silently he cursed their haste. Boots would have saved them time and possible frostbite out in the mountains, but there was no going back now. He made sure the others were following and pressed on.

Half an hour passed as they made their slow way up. The wind howled, threatening to hurl them from the rocky slope, but they continued, wings pulled tight around them. Briefly, Chris considered trying to use them, but dropped the thought just as quickly. Conditions were not ideal for a first attempt at flight.

When they finally reached the canyon mouth, Chris paused, glancing back as the other filed up behind him. One by one they joined him in the shadow beneath the cliffs. Within, the canyon twisted deeper into the mountains. A river flowed along its far side, and the roar of water echoed around them.

The hairs on Chris's neck tingled as he looked down the valley and saw black-garbed figures spilling from the facility. They gathered near the high walls, concentrating around several figures in white. Chris blinked, and the scene below came into sudden focus. It was as though a film had been removed from his eyes, and now the whole world was revealed to him in more detail than he could ever have imagined.

There was fear on the faces of the guards as they huddled close together, their rifles clutched tight. Blood and tears marked their clothing, and Chris wondered what exactly Angela had done to distract them.

His attention was drawn to the doctors standing with them. There was no sign of Halt, but he recognized Doctor Radly and Faulks. They didn't seem to have noticed Chris and the others yet, but it would only take one glance change that.

Silently, Chris waved for the others to get into cover, not trusting his voice, in case it carried down to those below. He scrambled up the last few feet of the gravel slope and dropped down into the canyon.

The others were quick to join him, coming over the lip one by one. They retreated behind the boulders lodged in the mouth of the pass, their eyes on Chris, waiting for him to speak.

Heart pounding in his chest, Chris slipped back out from behind the boulders. Crouching low, he half-crawled back up to the gravel lip. At the entrance to the pass, he dropped to his stomach and crawled the last few inches. There, he lifted his head and peered at the facility.

And immediately dropped back down.

36

C hris slammed his fist into the gravel, cursing their luck.

A few more seconds, and we would have been clear.

He slid down the slope to the others. Biting back his frustration, he only shook his head at their questioning looks. Below, a line of black figures were streaming up towards the canyon. They had been spotted. Now all they could do was flee, and hope to outrun their pursuers.

"They've seen us," he hissed. He began to thread his way through the boulders strewn across the canyon floor. "Let's go."

Gritting his teeth against the howling wind, Chris picked his way over the rocky ground, taking care to avoid patches of ice. The stones were slick, worn smooth by the passage of floodwaters, but at least they were gentler on his feet. Above them the canyon walls closed in, stretching up two, almost three hundred feet.

Rocks ground against one another as the others followed, shifting beneath their weight. To their right the river tumbled over its stony bed, roaring as it rushed down a series of cascades, making its slow journey through the twisting canyon. In the spring it would rise with the melting snow, filling the gorge, but still in the grips of winter, it remained thankfully low.

Chris's gaze carried up the valley, following the sheer walls as they twisted out of sight. He scanned the ground ahead, picking out a trail amidst the rock-strewn ground. He was quickly adapting to the weight of his wings. His muscles surged with a newfound energy, with the joy of freedom. Behind them the mouth of the canyon remained empty, but even so he picked up the pace, springing from stone to stone with hardly a pause between. Fear of the guards and their guns drove him on. Though they were moving at a good pace, their pursuers did not have to catch them—only set them in their rifle's sights.

Redoubling his efforts, Chris felt the granite cliffs press in around him. From somewhere ahead, the roar of water grew louder. Like distant thunder it drew him on, calling him deeper into the mountains. Sucking in great mouthfuls of damp air, Chris raced for the first bend in the canyon.

Boulders the size of cars littered the ground. Where the canyon narrowed they clustered in groups, almost blocking their passage. They scrambled over them one by one, slipping on the wet surfaces while the others watched, awaiting their turn.

Chris's ears tingled as a voice carried up the canyon. Acting on instinct, he grabbed Liz and pulled her behind a boulder, waving for the others to get down. An instant later the shriek of bullets tore the air, followed by the sharp *crack* of rock shattering. Cowering behind shelter, they watched as the boulder on which they'd just been standing disintegrated. Hot lead tore great chunks from the rock, turning smooth stone to pockmarks.

For a moment, Chris stood frozen, terrified by the sheer display of power. In his mind he saw himself caught by the bullets, saw his flesh tear and his bones shatter. Then Liz grasped him by the shoulder and shook him. He blinked, returning to the present to find her crystal eyes staring at him, just a few feet away.

On impulse he grabbed her by the waist and pulled her close. They kissed, hard and fast, the moment filled with a desperate passion, with the thrill of a chase. A second later they broke apart and turned to face the others. Richard raised an eyebrow, but Chris ignored him. The first bend in the canyon was close now, just a few more yards away. But in the open space they would be exposed to the guards and their unforgiving bullets.

Yet they had to move. No doubt men were already climbing towards them, growing closer with every passing second.

"We run for it," was all Chris said, before he turned and leapt from cover, unwilling to wait and see whether the others followed.

The buzz of bullets turned to a roar as he appeared from behind the boulder. Then he was racing across the open ground, stones slipping beneath his bare feet, faster than thought. With each step the shriek of bullets grew louder, as the guards far below adjusted their aim. Stone chips tore his flesh as the impact of bullets shook the ground beneath him. He ducked low, the hackles on his neck rising in anticipation of pain.

His wings snapped open, beating hard, driving him faster. He stumbled as he miscalculated his next jump, almost falling before recovering with a wild wave of arms. Liz bounded past, flashing him a sideways glance. But he was already up and beside her, pushing hard, his lungs burning not with exhaustion, but fear. Around him he heard the gasps of the others, their desperate, unintelligible cries.

And over it all, the screech of bullets.

Suddenly the air was clear, the cliff rising up to shield them from view. Together they drew to a stop, sucking in long mouthfuls of air, their eyes wild as they looked at each other, shocked and elated, thrilled by their survival.

They did not pause for long. They had won a respite, but they were still far from free. Ahead the canyon narrowed, the twists and turns coming closer together, and for the next thirty minutes they did not see their pursuers again. The rocks grew larger, until only boulders remained. They blocked the gorge, the creek threading its way between them, over and under, plunging ever down towards the hidden guards. The roar of water continued to grow, and the taste of the air changed, filling with moisture. In his mind, Chris pictured the stream cascading down into the canyon, and prayed it would offer them an escape.

He pressed on, drawing the others with him. The canyon floor grew steeper, winding up towards the clifftops high overhead. Their progress slowed, the going becoming more difficult. In places they were forced to backtrack where the way grew too steep, too treacherous to pass.

Finally, Chris bounded around the final bend in the canyon. The roar of water turned to a deafening thunder. His stride slowed as he took in the sight above. Beside him, Liz continued her upward march, her head down, eyes fixed on the ground. It was only when he reached out and grabbed her shoulder that she looked up, that she saw where he had led them.

❦ 37 ❦

C hris had not been wrong about the waterfall. Three hundred feet above their heads, a river rushed over the edge of the cliff and out into the void. Water filled the air, whirling as it was caught by the wind, turning it to a fine mist, to a light rain that fell all around them. At the base of the falls, the remains of the river crashed down onto a jagged pile of rocks. From there, the stream wound its way through the canyon to where the seven of them stood.

Beyond the waterfall, the canyon twisted back on itself, ending in a wall of sheer rock. A pile of rubble had accumulated against the cliff opposite the water-fall, stretching up almost two hundred feet. Straggly patches of vegetation sprouted from the rubble, fed by the ready source of water.

Chris closed his eyes, feeling the spray of water

on his cheeks, even where they stood several hundred feet away. It settled in his hair and trickled down his face, until he gave an angry shake of his head and wiped it away. He clenched his fists, shivering with cold and frustration.

There was no way they could climb those cliffs, no way they could reach the top before the bullets of the guards found them. He had led them to a dead end, into a trap. With the guards closing in, there was nowhere left to go.

Looking at the others, he saw his despair reflected in their faces. Only Ashley seemed undaunted. She walked up beside him, her eyes traveling up the canyon, to the pile of rubble. He turned, following her gaze, straining to see through the mist. Jagged boulders clustered around the top of the rubble, and the cliffs above them were cracked and broken. At some point, part of the cliff must have given way. There was no telling for sure, but from a distance it looked as though there was a crack they might be able to climb.

"Let's go," Ashley said, flashing him a smile as she took the lead.

Chris was glad to relinquish the position. The weight of failure hung heavy on his shoulders. The others did not speak, but he could feel the eyes of Jasmine and Richard on his back. Ahead, Ashley seemed to glide across the rocks, moving with a grace Chris wished he could match. She reached the rubble mound well before the rest of them and started up.

Following her, Chris only managed a few steps before the loose gravel slipped beneath his feet. He threw out an arm, grasping the branches of a disheveled bush, then screamed as thorns tore into his palm. Cursing, he regained his balance and released the bush, only then daring to look at his hand.

Dark marks spotted his palm, the broken thorn tips embedded deep in his flesh. Blood seeped from a dozen cuts and the skin was already turning red around the marks. He swore again, but there was little he could do about it now. Cradling his arm, he moved after Ashley.

The mist closed around them as they climbed, soaking them to the skin. Chris shivered as a drop of water ran down his back and caught in his feathers. A tingle ran up his spine as a thought came to him. The feathered appendages trembled in response.

Fly!

Chris shook his head, casting the idea back out into the void. With the winds roaring through the canyon, and the cliffs pressing close, it would be suicide.

As they neared the top of the mound, the wind picked up speed. It howled down over the cliffs to pummel at them, tearing at their wings and threatening to send them plummeting to the rocks far below. Above, the river continued its eternal plunge over the granite cliffs, filling the air with swirling clouds of water vapor.

A cry came from above. Chris looked up in time to see Ashley slip, then threw himself to the side as a rock bounced down towards him. He shouted a warning to the others, but thankfully they had spread out, and it tumbled harmlessly past them.

Recovering, Ashley continued her ascent, though Chris noticed she was favoring her left hand now. But she was already drawing level with the ring of boulders crowning the slope. Picking up his pace, Chris soon joined her at the base of the great rocks. Together they waited for the others to join them.

Once the seven had gathered on the narrow ledge, they turned to face the boulders. Here, Ashley took the lead again, squeezing in between two of the boulders. The way was narrow, and the extra bulk of their wings didn't help, but with a little difficulty, Chris managed to follow her. Ahead, the crevice ended at another boulder, but Ashley was already making short work of scrambling up, using the rocks on either side of her to climb.

Chris waited for her to reach the top before starting his ascent. The sharp pitch of the boulders and his injured hand made it difficult to find purchase. Cursing to himself, he pressed his back against one of the rocks to wedge himself in place, then levered himself up bit by bit using his arms and legs.

When he reached the top, Ashley was already gone. Following her wet footprints through the boulders, his optimism began to return. If they could wedge themselves into the crack in the cliff, they might be able to scramble up in the same way he had just managed. It would be a long and difficult haul—at least a hundred feet remained to be climbed—but it was better than waiting for the guards to catch them.

Chris stumbled as he emerged onto open ground. Realizing he was in the center of the ring of boulders, he looked around and found Ashley with her head pressed against the cliff, her fists clenched against the sheer stone. She turned as he approached, her eyes finding his.

His stomach twisted as Ashley slid down the wall until she sat, and covered her face with her hands. Her shoulders heaved as silent sobs shook her, tears spilling between her fingers.

Behind her the cliff stretched up another hundred feet, smooth and unmarked, the shadow they had thought was a crack no more than a change in the rock, a darker shade of granite.

They were trapped.

❦ 38 ❦

Liz paused as she emerged from the boulders and found Chris and Ashley slumped against the cliff. Their faces were ashen, their eyes despondent. In that instant, she knew they were finished. Her shoulders sagged, but she moved across to Chris and placed a hand on his head. He did not look up, just sat staring at the barren gravel.

Crouching, Liz pulled him to her chest. Stones rattled as Sam appeared beside her. He squatted by Ashley, whispering softly to her, pulling her up, getting her moving again. Trapped or not, there was no time to pause, to sit and wait for death to come for them.

"I'm sorry," Chris murmured.

Liz slid her fingers through his hair and down to his chin, turning his head to face her. "This isn't your fault, Chris. You were right, this was our best chance.

If we'd gone the other way, they would have already shot us dead. Now get up. We have to decide what to do next."

It took several tugs on Chris's arm before he gathered himself and stood. By then, Sam and Ashley looking more herself, though Liz suspected she was only wearing a brave face. But then, that's all any of them had left now.

"So, what now?" Jasmine crossed her arms, her eyes flashing as she looked around the circle. "I'm not going back."

Richard nodded his agreement.

Liz shivered, thinking of the guards creeping up the canyon towards them, of their black rifles shining in the afternoon light, promising death.

No, we can't go back.

To go back now would be worse than if they'd never escaped. They had tasted freedom, had rid themselves of the awful collars and breathed the fresh mountain air. And freezing though they were, with their wings drawn tight around their torsos, they were alive.

"There's nowhere left to go," Chris said, his voice cracking.

"Then we fight," Sam put in, his brow creased. Liz had never seen him so serious.

Around the circle, the others nodded, but Liz found herself shaking her head. Stepping past them, she climbed the nearest boulder, until she was perched atop it. She stared out over the gorge, peering through the swirling mist, seeking out their pursuers. The wind tore at her, sending her black hair flying across her face, but she ignored it.

She heard scuffling from behind her as the others climbed up, but did not turn. "What do you think?" she shouted over the wind.

Chris and the others gathered around her and looked out over the edge.

Chris swallowed and retreated a step, his eyes widening. The others stood in varying states of fear, though none were as close to the edge as Liz. To her right was the slope they'd just climbed, but directly beneath the boulder, the gravel fell away in a sheer drop, all the way to the canyon floor two hundred feet below.

Standing there, Liz felt no fear, only a silent resolve.

She would not go quietly back to her chains, to the cold cruelty of the doctors, to their needles and torture. She would not surrender to their bullets, to their harsh violence.

No, she would fight, she would resist, she would rage.

"You know," Ashley mused beside her, "they say birds just know. That their parents push them from the nest, and before they hit the ground, it comes to them."

"Care to go first?" Sam muttered.

Silence fell then as they each stared out over the canyon, watching as the tiny specks of the guards came into view. They crawled towards them like deadly ants, eyes searching the boulders strewn around them. Their gaze did not lift to where the seven of them stood, not yet.

Shivering, Liz looked at the others.

They looked back, waiting.

Turning to the edge, Liz took a deep breath. Movement came from beside her as Chris stepped forward, his fingers reaching out to entwine with hers. He glanced at her, his face drained of color. Naked fear looked out from his eyes, and she remembered his haunting climb up the training tower. Even so, he smiled.

"Just like baby birds, right?" He tried to laugh, but it came out more as a shriek.

Liz nodded, her stomach swirling. She closed her eyes, focusing on the foreign appendages on her back, feeling their presence, embracing them. They were still alien to her, a violation of her body…but she needed them now, needed to embrace them as a part of her.

Concentrating, Liz willed them to life.

With a *crack* of unfurling feathers, the great black expanse of her wings snapped open. The others gasped, but beside her Liz sensed movement. She smiled as Chris's tawny brown wings stretched out towards her own. A tremor shook her as their wingtips met, their feathers brushing together.

Liz flashed one last look back at the others. They wore wide grins on their face now, and their eyes were alive with excitement. She grinned back, and with Chris beside her, turned to face open air.

Together, they leapt out into the void.

❧ 39 ❧

C hris's stomach lurched into his chest as he plunged from the edge. The ground raced towards him at a terrifying speed, the jagged rocks looming large in his vision. His fear of falling realized, he opened his mouth and screamed.

Then his wings gave a sharp *crack* as they caught the air, and he was soaring, the wild wind catching in his twenty-four-foot wingspan, driving him up, up, up. His stomach twisted again, dropping sharply as the ground fell away. Chris let out another scream as he shot past the pale faces of his friends still standing atop the boulders.

The fear slid like Chris like water, and concentrating, he focused on turning, beating his wings to counter the powerful drafts swirling around him, and risked a wave to those below. The others waved back, then with only a moment's hesitation, they followed Chris and Liz off the cliff.

Chris swirled, his wings turning by what seemed to be a will of their own, and watched his friends plummet from the cluster of boulders. They dropped a dozen feet before their wings caught, halting their freefall and sending them hurtling back up into the sky. Broad grins split their faces, their eyes wild, their laughter echoing off the cliffs. In those briefest of moments, their hunters, their fears, all were forgotten. There was only the joy of flight.

But it could not last. An ache began in the center of Chris's back, and already he could feel the strain in his chest and abdomen, the muscles pulling tight to keep his wings moving. With their broad expanse, there seemed to be no need for giant wingbeats, but even the incremental adjustments of feathers and muscle was draining him. Looking at the others, he could see the strain beginning to affect them as well.

The mist swirled, providing them some cover from the guards below, or at least he hoped.

Sucking in a breath, he shouted across to the others, his words barely audible over the *thump* of wingbeats. "We have to fly over the cliffs!"

He had been studying the cliffs as the others gathered around him. They still towered overhead, their peaks tantalizingly out of reach. With the swirling winds hindering them, it would take a massive effort to climb those last hundred feet. He looked again for the guards and found them near the base of the rubble. They were looking up the slope, but they still had not spotted their winged prey.

After all, who would have guessed they could fly?

Returning his attention to the cliffs, Chris willed himself upwards. Muscles strained across his back and chest, his feathers shifted, and with a surge of elation he rose several feet. The others followed him, their faces creased with concentration, their eyes fixed on the ledge above. It wasn't far and still growing closer, but the winds were shifting, fighting against them. And as they neared the top, the raging waters grew closer, soaking them through, stealing away the last of their warmth.

Still they pressed on, their wings beating hard in the thin air. Water accumulated on their feathers, weighing them down. Chris's stomach tightened as muscles he'd never used stretched and twisted, driving his wings forward, sending him upwards.

Bit by bit, the top of the cliffs drew closer.

When they were still thirty feet away, Chris risked a glance down, and swore.

The guards were looking up at them, hands pointing, their eyes wide and mouths hanging open. Already one was dropping to his knee; others quickly followed suit. Rifles lifted to shoulders and a gun barrel flashed. In the open air, the seven of them presented an easy target.

By a will of their own, Chris's wings twisted,

sending him whirling sideways, even as he screamed at the others.

"Look out!"

Suddenly the air was alive with the screech of bullets. The others scattered like a flock of doves, flying outwards in all directions, though they strained to keep rising, to reach the clifftops, and safety.

Every inch of his body screaming, Chris drove himself on. Threads of terror wrapped their way around him, but somehow he found the strength to hold on. His wings worked by instinct now, alive with desperation, driven by the need to escape.

Abruptly he found himself in clear air. One instant the whiz of bullets and howling wind was all around him, then it was gone. Looking down, he realized he had made it, that he had crossed the threshold of the cliffs. The canyon had disappeared from view, dropping away as he shot over the icy ground a few feet below, still tracking the stream upwards.

Glancing back, he watched Sam shoot up over the lip of the cliff and then dive towards the ground, quickly followed by Jasmine and Richard. They evened out about thirty feet from the ground and raced towards where Chris was coming to a stop. They wore broad grins on their faces, though their cheeks were red and their breath billowed in clouds of vapor.

Chris looked past them, holding his breath, waiting for Ashley and Liz and the girl.

They appeared one by one, Liz first, then the girl, and finally, rising laboriously into sight, Ashley. Liz and the girl swept down towards them, but Ashley was struggling to maintain her height. Her wings were barely moving now, and her face was turning purple. She hovered over the lip of the cliff, drifting slowly towards them, driven by sheer determination.

Her eyes closed with sudden relief as she reached the clear air. Straightening out, her wings spread wide to catch the gentler breeze. A smile warmed her face as she looked across at them.

Then her smile faltered, her eyes widening as a shot echoed up from below. A red stain flowered on her chest and blood sprayed the air. Without a sound, Ashley's wings folded, and she plummeted to the icy ground.

❧ 40 ❧

Ashley lay in a tangled mess of limbs and feathers and wings, her flesh torn and broken, her face buried in snow. The only signs she lived came from the slow rise and fall of her back, the low gurgling from her chest. She coughed, half-rolling to reveal her battered face. Blood seeped from between her lips in a slow trickle, staining the snow beneath her.

She didn't move as they raced to her side. Her eyes were closed, and there was little chance she could be conscious after the fall. Chris was shocked she was even alive—though he wasn't sure if that was a blessing for her, or a curse. Her wings lay at awkward angles around her, and when he glanced at her legs he had to look away.

The bullet had taken her in the back and passed straight through her. Somehow it had missed her heart, but with the blood bubbling from her mouth, it appeared to have found a lung.

Another groan rattled from Ashley's chest, tearing at Chris's heart. He crossed the last few feet between them and crouched beside her. Tears built in his eyes, but angrily he wiped them away. He grasped Ashley's hand and gave it a gentle squeeze.

"Ashley," he whispered as the others gathered around them. "Ashley, it's okay, we're here."

Ashley. Brave, bold, elegant. When he'd first laid eyes on her, he'd thought her fragile, a sheltered city girl incapable of standing up for herself. She had put those misconceptions to rest with her first words. And time and time again since. She had proven herself stronger than any of them, her will unquenchable.

And now she lay here on the side of a mountain, her blood staining the frozen earth, and there was nothing any of them could do to help her.

She was dying.

Stones crunched as Sam crouched beside him, tears streaming down his face. Stretching out a tentative hand, he wiped the blood from Ashley's lips, as though that simple act might wake her, might bring her back to them. A sob tore from his throat as a fresh bubble of blood rose between her lips and burst.

He reached for her, as though to draw her into his arms, and then stopped. He knelt there with one arm outstretched, torn between his desperation to help her, and the fear he would only hurt her further.

The others stood around in silence, each lost in their own thoughts.

Long minutes dragged by as they watched her struggle, her every breath a desperate battle. They had time to spare now, though in truth all thought of escape had vanished. On the snowy plateau, they sat by their friend and watched her life slipping away.

As minutes ticked towards an hour, Ashley still clung to life. Her body was torn and broken, her lifeblood staining the snow red, but still she breathed, still she fought on.

Finally, Chris knew they could wait no longer. Sucking in a breath, he stood. Tears stung his eyes as Liz joined him, sliding an arm beneath his shoulder. He looked at the others, saw the indecision in even Jasmine and Richard's eyes. They could not stand here waiting for Ashley to die. And yet, they could not abandon her, could not let her last moments on this earth pass alone on this harsh mountainside.

He looked at the others, hating the question in their eyes. They wanted him to make a decision, though he was not sure when he'd become their leader. It felt strange, especially given Richard and Jasmine's animosity. But there was no time to debate it now.

"We can carry her," Chris whispered at last.

"No," Sam croaked, surprising him. The young

man looked up at Chris, his eyes red with tears, and shook his head. "No, you can't bring her with you. She'll only slow you down."

"We can't leave her," Liz said.

Sam closed his eyes, a shudder going through him. "I know," he breathed.

Chris stared at him, a tightness growing in his stomach. "What are you saying, Sam?"

"Go, Chris." Resolve shone in Sam's eyes now. "Go. Take the others with you. Leave, fly away from here, be free. I'll look after her." His voice broke as he finished, but there was steel in his words.

Looking at Sam, Chris wondered at the young man's courage. He opened his mouth to argue, to convince his friend to come with them, that they could carry Ashley, could keep her comfortable until…

"Maybe they can save her…" Sam finished.

With those five words, Chris realized they would never change Sam's mind. He meant to sacrifice himself for Ashley. He would give away his freedom, his life even, if there was the slightest chance she might live. Looking at her, Chris tried and failed to summon the same hope. Between the bullet and the fall, there was little left of the graceful girl he had known.

Yet still Ashley fought on, her iron will unyielding. Thinking of the miracles the facility had performed on them, he wondered if Sam might be right.

At last he nodded. In his arms, Liz began to tremble, but he pulled her tight before she could try to argue. She glanced at him, anger burning in her eyes, but he only shook his head.

This was Sam's decision to make. His alone.

Jasmine and Richard shared a glance. Whatever their history with Ashley and Sam, Chris doubted they had ever wished for this. Perhaps they would even miss his light-hearted presence.

"Good luck, Sam," Chris said, swallowing hard.

Sam nodded and then turned back to Ashley. With the utmost care, he slid his hands beneath her back and lifted her into his arms. She gave a tiny groan as she left the ground, seeming to shrink into Sam's massive frame. Her head lifted, her eyelids fluttering, before she nestled into the crook of Sam's arm and still once more.

Gently, Jasmine and Richard helped tuck the shattered mess of Ashley's wings into Sam's arms. Then they stood in silence as Sam moved back towards the cliffs. His copper wings slowly spread as he walked, his back straight, his gaze fixed straight ahead. He did not look back as he reached the edge. Without hesitating, stepped out into open air.

They stood for a moment after he had disappeared, waiting for the gunfire, praying he would reach the ground safely. But they did not go to the edge. They did not watch.

Chris didn't know about the others, but he could not bear to see Sam return to his chains.

Finally, Chris wiped away his tears and faced the others. They stood shivering in the cold mountain air, their eyes red, their faces pale. He could see the questions on their lips, but there was only one thing left for them to do now.

Fly.

❦ 41 ❦

The *Chead* paused in the doorway, momentarily blinded by the light streaming down from the infinite expanse stretching up above its head. Scraping noises came from behind it as the survivors of its pack shuffled forward, eager to take their first steps out into the world beyond.

They had fought hard, the *Chead* and its brethren. The men who'd stood against them had been feeble, weak creatures that broke easily. The first had died screaming as the *Chead* had rushed from their cages to tear them limb from limb. More death had followed as the nine *Chead* rampaged through the facility, eager for retribution against their tormentors.

Yet few of the hated white coats had fallen into their clutches, and eventually the humans had organized themselves, pinning the *Chead* and its brethren down with their foul weapons. The first of them had died, then another. Finally they had been forced to retreat, though the humans had not yet gathered the courage to follow.

The *Chead* smiled at the thought, its heart beginning to race. Its gaze swept the jagged earth rising up around the facility, the boulders and crevices offering them concealment. If the humans came after them, if they tried to hunt them down...

It paused as it caught the scent of humanity in the air. Turning, it stared up at the jagged slope above them. The grey and white of snow and rock appeared empty. There was no movement, no sign of life, and yet the *Chead* knew the humans were there, hidden somewhere in the twisting cliffs. It licked its lips, laughter building in its chest.

The other *Chead* gathered nearby, their grey eyes intent on the cliffs, their ears twitching at the distant *clacking* of stones shifting beneath human feet. Smiles crossed their lips as they looked to their leader, awaiting his decision.

The *Chead* was about to lift its hand, when it scented something else. It paused, breathing it in, tasting the strange sweetness to it, familiar, and yet unmistakably different from the feeble humans. The others stirred, impatient for the hunt, for the kill.

Still, their leader hesitated. Memories stirred as it recalled the strange creatures it had fought so many weeks ago. It frowned, seeing again the battle, the desperation of its foes as they sought to fight back.

Their defiance had driven the *Chead* into a familiar fury, one which no enemy could hope to survive.

Yet the strange creatures had lived. They had not been *Chead*, but together the boy and girl had possessed a strength far beyond their human captors. Together, they had defeated it.

The *Chead* shivered, just the memory threatening to ignite its fury. It drew in a long breath of the icy air, seeking calm. The jagged earth up around them promised freedom, if only they kept their minds. It could not afford to surrender to the rage now, not when they were so close.

Distantly, the *Chead* recalled what had come next. The traitor in the white coat had demanded the *Chead's* death, had tortured the strange creatures to force them to its will.

And they had refused.

The *Chead's* ears twitched as a gunshot rang from the cliffs. More followed, echoing down the valley to where the *Chead* stood.

The hunt begins, the *Chead* thought as it watched the mountains.

The humans no longer seemed interested in the escaped *Chead*. They had found new prey. Glancing down the valley, the *Chead* contemplated the empty ground, the freedom it offered. Another *boom* drew its gaze back to the mountains. A distant scream whispered in its mind, as it saw again the boy standing in defiance of the traitor, and the girl writhing on the ground.

Letting out a long breath, the *Chead* started up the slope.

With a crunch of gravel, the others followed.

Phase One: Complete
The story continues in…
The Pursuit of Truth

ENJOYED THIS BOOK?

I hope so! This book was just a little different from my usual fantasy stuff, so it's not exactly everyone's cup of tea (sorry bit of slang us kiwis picked up from the English). Anyway! If you did enjoy the book, be sure to read on with part two: The Pursuit of Truth. You could also leave this book a review on Amazon if you'd like to see more of this kind of story from me!

FOLLOW AARON HODGES...
And receive TWO FREE novels and a short story!
www.aaronhodges.co.nz/newsletter-signup/

THE SWORD OF LIGHT TRILOGY

If you've enjoyed this book, you might want to check out my very first fantasy series!

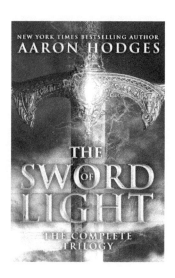

A town burns and flames light the night sky. Hunted and alone, seventeen year old Eric flees through the wreckage. The mob grows closer, baying for the blood of their tormentor. Guilt weighs on his soul, but he cannot stop, cannot turn back. **If he stops, they die.**